The Expats

The Expats

Skeletons in the Cupboard Series Book 5

A.J. Griffiths-Jones

In Loving Memory of Phil Pimlott
1973 - 2016

Author's Note

As the world reached a new millennium at the turn of the 21st Century, more and more skilled workers were seeking employment overseas, reaching out to unique opportunities and grasping them with both hands.

Unlike foreign traders and prospectors in previous years who had ventured out, leaving their families safely at home, this new breed of employee were uprooting their wives and children and embarking on a new life in faraway lands.

My husband and I were just two of those foreigners seeking to make our fortune in a new country. His career as a talented engineer had opened unexpected doors and in 2003 we embarked upon the adventure of a lifetime. I wasn't worried about finding work, as we packed up our belongings and prepared to fly to Asia, as I had plenty of teaching experience and relished the challenges that lay before us. It was hard saying goodbye to family and friends, wondering if we were making the right decision and contemplating who would come to visit us and when, but the excitement of beginning a new adventure together far outweighed any fears that we may have had and hence the journey began.

This tale is based upon our experiences and friendships forged in Shanghai, China, where we initially agreed to spend two years but ended up staying for a decade. The city was, and still is, a vibrant melting pot of people from all walks of life and we met some wonderful people both Chinese and other nationalities from around the globe, making it hard to tear ourselves away when the time came to leave, but also content in the knowledge that we had created many wonderful memories.

Some of the chapters in this work of fiction are based on true events but the characters are, for the most part, pure figments of my very over-active imagination. I know that our friends won't mind me sharing their pieces of this very colourful jigsaw puzzle, as they know that they all have a very special place in our hearts, we all have the photos, and in some cases scars, to prove it.

If you ever find yourself wondering whether you should take the plunge and seek a position overseas, I can only advise that you take it. Living and working in Shanghai was amazing and it has given me the tools to live a fearless and eventful life. This book is dedicated to every person who shared a slice of Shanghai life with us and never ever forgetting the one who didn't come home.

Contents

Prologue

Shanghai. A vast sprawling metropolis divided down its centre by the mighty Huangpu river with Pu Dong (River East) and Pu Xi (River West) both dominating the skyline on either side with a myriad of old and new buildings, quite a sight to behold. Pu Dong holds the large housing estates, leafy avenues and industrial zones, all newly forged on recently acquired land, much to the bewilderment of the generations who have watched the skyscrapers rise up where their ancestor's farms once lay in peace and tranquility. On the other side is Pu Xi, another busy hive of activity where old and new buildings sit side by side, each blind to the other's origins and where millions of commuters come bustling every day to try their luck in business, whether it be in the world of high-level commerce or selling cheap souvenirs to the tourists that flock here daily, hoping to catch a glimpse of Shanghai's colourful past.

The Bund (Waterfront) serves as a reminder of the Lao Wai (foreigners) who came here last century, opening banks, setting up trading posts and igniting the flames of the opium wars, turning this city into the Paris of the East, a place where everyone wanted to venture and where virtually anything could be bought, at a price.

Modern day Shanghai is still as enticing as its historical counterpart although stark contrasts exist at every turn. Champagne brunch in each of the top hotels is a weekly occurrence, where free-flow alcohol and every type of food you could imagine can be tried for a set price, whilst listening to classical music by talented musicians and entertained by top-class acrobatic performers, all the time being waited upon by servers who return home to their meagre apartments after spending their working hours observing in wonderment how the other half live.

The Chinese nationals are a curious race, naturally inquisitive to learn about the foreigners who come to live in their land and bemused by their odd habits and customs. One such example is the Chinese attitude towards mealtimes, unable to understand a foreign worker eating as and when he has time or feels hungry, whereas a local will eat at the exact same time every day, believing firmly that a body needs regularity and will suffer dire consequences if it is not sustained by ritual. Also we have, for hundreds of years, cited our unlucky number as thirteen, whereas in China it is the number four, as the sound 'Si' is the same as the word 'Si' meaning death.

Embarking on a relocation to Shanghai was, and still is, far easier than a move to many other Asian cities. Homes are equipped with all mod-cons, in a fashion, and almost anything can be ordered and delivered to your door for a small fee.

However, charges also apply to emergency services whose ambulance drivers will refuse to deliver you safely to a hospital until the requisite amount is paid, no matter how severe the medical need.

Traffic is crazy and foreigners are discouraged from driving for their own safety, although taking a taxi can be a harrowing experience too with drivers frequently taking long routes unless you are sure of your destination and, on occasion, falling asleep at the wheel due to long unmonitored working hours. On the fun side, you are just as likely to see a man cycling down the road with a freezer strapped to his bike as to come up alongside a person on a scooter with a whole pig on the back. Expect the unexpected.

Food is something that should be questioned frequently. Korean and Northern Chinese restaurants in Shanghai serve up roasted dog meat, and open-air markets sell produce which hasn't been refrigerated and are exposed to all the elements. Local dishes are prepared with care and expertise although none taste like those we have come to know at home, where Asian chefs concoct Western versions to suit our less adventurous palates. Sometimes, however, it's the little things that you might really miss. Imagine living in a place where you can buy chocolate bread on every corner but a sugar-free loaf is nowhere to be found and a tin of baked beans costs more than a haircut at the barbers.

There is so much to explore in this place, from the mesmerising acts at 'Circus World', where eight motorcyclists ride perilously together inside a giant dome, to watching parents of single Shanghainese children tout for prospective partners in People's Park, hanging photographs and personal details on the bushes in the hope that a match can be found.

Of course nowadays, the foreign wives or Tai Tai's (mistresses) have it easier. With leading fashion retailers from the West setting up stores in the city it has become less of a struggle to make purchases, unlike the days where shopping for new underwear would involve being groped by the shop assistant as they attempted to guess your measurements and produce items more fitting for your age than to be deemed as sexy. Gone too are the days when you would cross the threshold of a shop to be told they had nothing in your size, such has Shanghai evolved.

Imagine yourself now, embarking on a journey into the unknown, with little grasp of the Mandarin language and the few words that you have managed to remember rendered useless within the realms of the Shanghainese dialect. The city is alive, bursting with inhabitants whose numbers total more than some small countries, a vast and dangerous playground for the very rich and the very poor alike. Shanghai is capable of so many things. It can create fortunes, make or break relationships and implant the deepest of memories. For me, it will always be my second home.

Chapter One

Li Yang

"Ni hao."

Li Yang called out in Mandarin, greeting her husband as she pushed the front door to their tiny apartment closed with her foot, whilst balancing a huge nylon bag in her arms. It had been a long day and the middle-aged woman desperately longed to sit with her feet in a bowl of warm water, but there was still dinner to prepare, washing to do and a pile of socks to darn.

"Ni hao ma (How are you?)" Xu Wei asked sleepily as he trudged into the hallway to relieve his wife of her heavy burden, his slippers scraping across the tiled floor as he walked.

Li Yang quickly gave him a run-down of her day in rapid-fire Shanghainese, emphasising how tired she was but still excited to show him the goodies that her departing employers had bestowed upon her. Most of the contents of her chequered nylon holdall were foodstuffs that the family couldn't take with them overseas but there were also several items of clothing and some decorative cushion covers.

Xu Wei peered into the bag and pulled out a large sachet of rose tea, "Why do these foreigners buy such large quantities of everything?" he pondered, as his wife took the packet and inhaled the aroma, "Such a lot of waste. We Chinese have more sense, to buy what you need fresh from the market every day."

Li Yang smiled, she too could never understand the Lao Wai and their unusual habits, but it was the foreign community in the city who had ensured her continuous employment over the years. Some had been easier to get along with than others and a few had been very strict about working hours and the finicky way in which they liked their homes cleaned but overall the benefits had outweighed the downfalls.

4

"I expect your new employers will be glad to have someone of your experience to help them," Xu Wei muttered as he poured water from the dispenser to make his wife a drink, "You start tomorrow, don't you?"

Li Yang nodded and took out vegetables from a small carrier bag that she had hooked over her arm, "Yes, they're from England and have a young daughter, so I expect they will want me to work some evenings too. I'm looking forward to it."

Xu Wei smiled, there was always a little extra cash when his spouse worked longer hours which would be very useful soon, as their son was approaching an age where he should be married and having a child.

"What are we having to eat?" he sniffed, "I'm very hungry."

Li Yang rolled her eyes and pulled a second bag from inside the first, it contained chicken wings.

"I'll make them hot and spicy, just how you like," she told the man at her side, "You can put on some rice."

As preparations for their dinner commenced, the woman reflected upon the many differences between her own race and the Westerners who came to live in Shanghai, such as the simplicity of eating rice. In her culture, the rice was eaten after the main course, as something to fill you up if you were still hungry but, with her employers, they mixed the two dishes together on one plate regardless of the diverse texture and flavours. She knew that Chinese food was served that way overseas, her employers had never tired of telling her, but still it seemed a strange combination.

"Look at this huge packet of mixed spice," Xu Wei was saying, pulling another pouch out of the bag, causing his wife to turn around, "This would take us over a year to finish. Shall I take some for our neighbor?"

Li Yang nodded and continued her task of heating oil in a wok, so much waste, she thought, it's crazy.

Later, after having eaten and cleared away the dishes, the couple sat contentedly in front of their television set but neither person was watching the news programme that aired in the background. Li Yang was mending socks and thinking about the new arrivals while the man that she loved so dearly snoozed peacefully in his armchair, a toothpick still clutched between his fingers and his trousers undone to let his stomach relax from the hearty meal he had just eaten.

Li Yang wasn't concerned about meeting her new Lao Wai family, the wife had seemed very friendly when she had been introduced by the Ayi agency a couple of weeks before, but you never knew how people would behave behind their own closed doors. An Australian woman that she had worked for some time ago had been depressed about moving to China, not knowing anyone and miles away from her family, and had taken up the habit of following Li Yang around the house with a mug in her hand as the Chinese woman cleaned. It turned out that there was wine in the mug and by teatime the woman would be fast asleep on the sofa, the empty bottles cleared miraculously away and her unsuspecting husband none the wiser. Of course, Li Yang knew that not all foreign women were like that, but she knew that most of them liked to go and drink at the weekends, although their insane shopping habits were worse than their wine imbibing ones. She was sure that this new foreign woman would reveal her bad habits eventually as a cleaning lady usually saw the worst of things, especially first thing in the morning. Except for the Germans, Li Yang smiled, never had she witnessed a cross word, the remains of a wild party or tension between a couple while working for that particular race, although they were very strict on the upkeep of their homes.

"Cha ma (Tea?)" Xu Wei asked, stirring his wife from her thoughts, "I'll make it."

Li Yang set aside the darning and followed her husband into the kitchen, eager to put away the rest of the goods given to her that day, in particular she wanted to show him the gift that her employers had given her as a token of their appreciation. It was wrapped in pink tissue paper, and bubble wrap inside that, for protection.

"Can can (look)" she smiled, unwrapping the delicate object and placing it on the table.

"Bu hao," Xu Wei scorned, frowning at the little glass clock that his wife was admiring so longingly, "That's very bad. Don't they know that we never give clocks as a gift, it means the time of your death will come rapidly, how thoughtless."

"Mei wen ti (no problem)" Yang soothed, rubbing his arm, "These foreigners don't know our customs, besides Tai Tai Brenda was only here for a short while."

Xu Wei shrugged, but his unhappy expression didn't change, "I suppose it will be useful," he relented, "But these people really should have more sense about such things."

Li Yang took her husband's concession as consent and took the clock through to their bedroom where she placed it on the bedside cabinet. Now she wouldn't have to listen to the dreadful tune on Xu Wei's mobile phone that woke them up every morning, this clock had a delicate ring that would be much kinder to their ears.

"Cha," the Chinese man called, setting his wife's tea down beside her armchair.

Li Yang returned to the living room and looked around. She was content with their small apartment, it was neat and big enough for the three of them, although their son was often out with his friends but, on the odd occasion, she did wonder what it would be like to live in one of the grand homes that her employers could afford. It seemed that they always had more rooms than they needed and were forever buying things to furnish their lavish interiors. She had known couples with no children living in three or four-bedroom homes, keeping the rooms aired and fresh for visiting friends and family. There was no need to do such a thing in her home, the woman smiled, family lived close by, and anyway, she wouldn't dream of living such an extravagant lifestyle, not that their combined income would ever cover such a luxury.

"What is it?" Xu Wei sniffed, looking up inquisitively from his seat, "Are you daydreaming again?"

Li Yang smiled, he knew her too well, "Not really husband, I am just wondering about tomorrow."

Next morning, the couple rose from their bed bright and early. Xu Wei started his factory job at eight o'clock but he had an hour commute across the city to get there and liked to do some gentle exercise before starting his shift. Li Yang ushered him out through the door before making herself some lunch to reheat at her new job, leftover chicken and vegetables would fill her up perfectly. Her husband was lucky that his meals were provided by the company that employed him. Sometimes Li Yang had found kindly employees who insisted on her taking lunch in their kitchen but mostly the food consisted of sandwiches which the Chinese woman didn't consider substantial, especially in the winter months when something warm was needed to sustain a healthy body. It would only take the ayi, or housekeeper, fifteen minutes to ride her scooter to the gated complex where she would begin her new position but Li Yang wanted to call at her friend's home first and collect a small offering for the new Tai Tai (mistress).

Deng Ping lived in a row of tiny cottages which used to be part of a very pros-perous farm in days gone by, but now the buildings had become surrounded by multi-million Yuan high-rise complexes and they all knew that it wouldn't be long before the Chinese government made a compulsory purchase order to evict the tenants and sell the land to developers.

"Ni hao," Deng Ping called from the doorway as her friend dismounted and leaned the scooter up against an outside wall, "Ni chi le ma (Have you eaten?)"

Li Yang replied in the affirmative, it was customary for friends to ask each other if they had eaten and if the response was negative, they would be taken inside to have a snack or meal, depending on the time of day. Having eaten a steamed bun for breakfast, Li Yang was content.

"Have you come for some eggs?" Deng Ping smiled, leading her friend around to the back of the cottage where dozens of chickens roamed about the yard, "They're fresh."

"Shi er ma?" Li Yang asked, wondering if it would be alright to have a dozen, "Thank you Ping."

Deng Ping took a cardboard carton from a stack by the chicken run and then gently knelt down to feel around in the straw for the perfectly formed eggs that her precious hens had laid.

It was ten minutes to eight when Li Yang switched off her engine and care-fully lifted the tray of eggs from their resting place in the basket on the front of her scooter. Not one was broken, the sign of a smooth ride and a fortuitous sign that her new position would be a positive one.

Riding up three floors in the lift, the cleaning lady studied her own reflection in the mirrored glass. She didn't look bad for a woman in her mid-fifties but had aged considerably in the past couple of years. Li Yang tucked a stray wisp of grey hair behind her ear with one hand, carefully hugging the eggs with the other until the lift stopped and the doors opened opposite apartment 301.

The ayi knocked gently and stood listening for footsteps.

"Hello," the cheery faced householder beamed, "Come on in."

Li Yang nodded and slipped off her shoes before following the auburn-haired, buxom foreign woman down the hallway and into a bright, spacious lounge.

"Sorry, what should I call you?" the woman was asking as her new cleaner looked around with wide eyes.

Li Yang looked back blankly, "Sorry, little English," she murmured.

"I'm Delia," the woman said slowly, patting her own chest in an attempt to explain.

"Li Yang," the Chinese woman replied, suddenly realising what was being asked.

"I know, what I mean is should I call you Li?" the foreigner prompted. Li Yang shook her head, "Yang, please. Li is family name."

Delia nodded and repeated the name Yang a couple of times before gesturing towards the kitchen.

Li Yang offered the eggs forward and smiled, "For you."

"Oh thank you!" Delia gushed, taking the cardboard tray, "How very kind."

The ayi noticed that her new employer laughed nervously every time she spoke but her eyes sparkled as though she were privy to some joke that nobody else knew about. They would get along very well the Chinese woman thought. Just as Delia opened a cupboard to show Yang her vast array of cleaning products, there was a thud behind them, forcing both women to turn around.

The cheekiest little girl stood grinning at them and Yang's heart began to melt.

"This is Peggy," Delia grinned, pulling her little girl into the room, "Say hello to Yang sweetheart."

"Hello," the youngster smiled shyly, trying to hide behind her mother.

"Hen piao lian (very pretty)", Yang sighed, letting out her breath, "Hello."

By mid-day it had become apparent to Li Yang that Mistress Delia didn't work and stayed home to take care of her daughter. She knew that child-care during the day hadn't been a part of their original agreement but she really wouldn't have minded looking after Peggy, as she was such an adorable child.

At one o'clock Delia breezed into the kitchen with her daughter in tow. Her new employee was cleaning the glass doors that led out onto a small balcony and smiled briefly before continuing her task.

"Would you like a sandwich Yang?" Delia asked, pointing at bread and ham that she'd put onto the worktop.

"Oh, no," Yang spluttered, hoping that she wasn't expected to eat a heavy lunch with her new Tai Tai, "I have." She opened the fridge and pointed to her plastic lunchbox which she would need to microwave.

"Okay, if you're sure," Delia shrugged, slathering butter on the crusty loaf, "Coffee?"

Yang Li shook her head "Sui," she said pointing to the water dispenser.

There was little more that could be said regarding lunch after that brief exchange, each woman realising that they would have to grasp more of the other's language if life were to progress smoothly in this household but each satisfied that they could get along well in a very amicable way.

Delia called to her daughter to sit at the dining table to eat her sandwich while Li Yang put away the dirty cloths and heated up her own lunch to eat at the breakfast bar. She had been working at a steady pace since nine that morning and was feeling quite peckish. It wouldn't be too bad here, she thought, although generally houses were easier to look after when the Tai Tai left the ayi to her own devices, and already that morning Delia had pointed out that Li Yang wasn't using the correct cleaning products for certain tasks. It was obvious that this employee was going to be quite particular, the housekeeper mused as she ate the chicken wings, so to avoid any unnecessary conflict the ayi would have to make notes on how Delia liked things doing and try her best to remember.

Still, she thought, Peggy looked a bundle of fun and at just three years old it would be easy to teach her some Chinese words, hopefully leading to a firm bond between them.

The day progressed slowly, with Delia unpacking boxes of their shipped belongings and Li Yang moving from room to room getting the basic cleaning done, such as floors, windows and skirting boards.

Peggy seemed content to watch cartoons on the television while her mother decided where to put this vase or that bowl, but Li Yang kept popping her head around the living room door to make sure that the little one was alright. A good start overall to a new situation and the ayi felt confident that she could settle.

Arriving home that evening, Li Yang was pleased to see that her husband had already started preparing dinner, not a rare occurrence but something that he did less and less as he grew older.

"Ni hao," Xu Wei called as soon as he heard the door latch click, "How was everything?"

"Hen hao (very good)," his wife smiled, entering the kitchen, "The Tai Tai is quite nice, a little bit picky but at least she doesn't follow me around checking what I'm doing like some of them."

Xu Wei nodded, "That's good, is she very young?"

The Chinese woman shrugged, "I don't know, it's hard to tell with these foreign women, I suppose she's in her thirties. What are you making?"

Her husband lifted the lid on a steamer, revealing a whole fish surrounded by green vegetables.

"Mmm, smells good," Li Yang told him, wafting the fragrant steam across the room and inhaling deeply.

"Sit down," Xu Wei instructed, "Ready in two minutes."

As the couple sat finishing their meal, the front door opened and closed with a loud bang.

"Ni hao," a young man grinned as he entered the room.

"Ni chi le ma (have you eaten?)" Xu Wei asked, immediately getting up to greet his son.

"Chi le," the twenty-three-year-old answered, confirming that he had indeed eaten.

"Na li (where?) Xu Bo," Li Yang asked, concerned that her only child had been eating junk food.

Xu Bo rolled his eyes and flopped down onto one of the kitchen chairs, "KFC."

There followed a great deal of fast-talking Shanghainese, as both parents quizzed their son on exactly what he had eaten and why, emphasising strongly that such food choices were not good for a Chinese boy. The topic of conversation was only drawn to a close after Xu Bo promised to eat at home with his parents the following evening.

"I've been working so hard," the young man complained, "Our boss is pushing us to sell more these days but people don't have the money to buy large electrical goods very often."

Li Yang nodded, she knew from her family's own personal experience that it was hard to afford the luxuries that some people took for granted. She would have loved a modern washing-machine or a television set with a bigger screen, but their main focus these days was to ensure that Xu Bo found a suitable partner and got married before he was twenty-five. It didn't matter that he couldn't afford rent on an apartment on his current salary, as his new wife could move in with the family, such situations were perfectly normal in Eastern culture.

Xu Wei belched loudly and pushed his empty plate away from him, "Your mother started her new job today, aren't you interested to hear about it?"

"Of course," Xu Bo grinned, taking Li Yang's hand, "How was it? Are they rich? Is their home large?"

His father tutted to show his disapproval of his son's questions, "All you young people think about is money. It is much more important to be happy than rich Xu Bo."

The young man laughed, "We live in a vast city father, where the very rich and the very poor live side by side. Don't you hope to make a fortune some day?"

Li Yang scoffed, ruffling her son's hair, "There is no chance at our old age, we must be content with our modest home and good health, now go and take off your work clothes while I make some tea."

Xu Bo retreated to his bedroom, banging the door carelessly as he went and within seconds loud pop music could be heard coming from a transistor radio.

Xu Wei touched Li Yang's shoulder gently, "Don't worry, when we find a match for him, everything will change. He will have a child of his own and become responsible."

His wife nodded hopefully, "Perhaps we can find him a young woman with good prospects, maybe the daughter of a business owner or tradesman."

Unaware of his parents discussing their plans to marry him off, Xu Bo was lying on his bed reading a magazine that he had purchased that afternoon on his break. He knew that his parents would be very disappointed if they knew their son had been wasting money on such frivolous things, and kept a watchful eye on the door, ready to stuff the glossy pages under his pillow should either of them enter. The Shanghainese youngster had a vision of how to become more affluent and this journal, full of fashion and fast cars was only just the beginning.

An hour or so later, Xu Bo took his grubby work shirt through to the balcony where his mother was hanging up washing, and asked her if she could wash it for him.

"You have two other blue shirts for your job," Li Yang chided him, "Wear one of those."

"But this one fits better mother," her son complained, "The others are too tight."

Li Yang looked the young man up and down, as he stood in a pair of boxer shorts and a white vest, hair flattened at the back from lying down and a cheeky grin on his face.

"You're putting on weight," she scolded, "Xu Bo you must stop eating fast food with your friends, come home and eat with your father and me, like a good son. Besides, you shouldn't waste your money."

The young man stifled a yawn and raised his hand in the air as he went back inside, "Okay."

Li Yang followed and tapped her husband on the shoulder as their son walked through the living room.

"See how Xu Bo is getting fat," she remarked candidly, "No girl will marry such an unhealthy boy."

Xu Wei nodded, trying to keep neutral ground between their only son and his beloved Li Yang. In the first years of their marriage it had been hard adhering to the Chinese government's one child policy, but they would never have been able to afford a second baby anyway on such meagre wages. Li Yang's sister had given birth to twins and everyone in the family was aware of the hardship that they had endured having to feed, school and clothe two children. The system was designed to control the population but, in some cases, it had caused unnecessary debt and oppression.

"Xu Bo," the elder man shouted as his son retreated back to his bedroom, "Listen to your mother."

The youngster closed his door once again and let out a sigh of disgust.

For the first two weeks in Li Yang's new position working for Tai Tai Delia, everything was fine. Initially there had been a fair amount of sign language and pot luck as the two women struggled with everyday communication but after a fortnight, things had settled into a routine.

Li Yang understood that Delia liked the beds to be changed every week, regardless of whether Yang thought they were dirty or not, and she also expected her cleaning lady to use different products for different jobs, a strange phenomenon for a Chinese woman whose home was swept with a broom and wiped down with warm water. Li Yang had been a great use to the new arrival too. Delia had never been out to buy fruit or vegetables locally, instead preferring the high-end foreign supermarket which cost three times the price. When the ayi had first broached the subject of shopping for Delia, she hadn't been able to make the suggestion clearly enough in English and the other woman had thought that Li Yang was offering to take her there. Before the confusion could be righted, Delia had strapped Peggy into her pushchair and smiled at Li Yang expectantly.

"Market?" she smiled, "Shall we go now Yang?"

Li Yang nodded and slipped on her pink anorak, this was going to be interesting, she thought.

Chinese open markets are both a joy and a curse, being full of fresh delicious produce which has no method of being put on ice or protected from predatory insects. The result can be eye-opening to say the least. Delia was about to get her first taste of life amongst the locals.

"Fish," Peggy chuckled from her seat as Delia pushed her through the cluster of stalls.

"Do they have prawns?" Delia asked, turning to her housekeeper expectantly.

Li Yang thought for a moment, unsure of what was being asked, "Fish here," she ventured.

"Oh it's okay, there they are," Delia suddenly exclaimed, excitedly pointing at a bowl of seafood.

Li Yang shook her head at the cooked prawns and pointed at some fresh ones, "This better Tai Tai."

Delia looked unsure but trusted the local woman's judgment, taking a note from her purse and gently putting it into Li Yang's hand.

On arriving back home, laden with all manner of fruit and vegetables, the housekeeper put away the produce before turning her attention to the prawns, which were bobbing around in a bag. She tipped them into a plastic bowl and filled it with water just as Delia came into the kitchen with her daughter.

"Eek," she squirmed, pointing at the shellfish, "They're still alive."

Li Yang looked down into the bowl, expecting to see something dreadful, "Tai Tai?" she asked.

"How am I supposed to cook those?" Delia gasped, "I can't kill them." "Yang cook," the ayi offered, pulling a wok from the cupboard.

The foreigner nodded and left the room, unable to contemplate what was about to happen.

On regaling her husband with the day's adventure, Li Yang couldn't help but chuckle, it had been the strangest incident she'd ever encountered.

"So, did they eat the prawns?" Xu Wei pressed, his eyes wide in disbelief.

"No!" the woman exclaimed, pulling open a large plastic tub, "She gave them to me to bring home."

The man also started to laugh then, "So, do you mean that foreigners would rather buy dead prawns or cooked ones than healthy fresh, live ones?"

"Yes, isn't it just the craziest thing you've ever heard?"

Xu Wei nodded, his fingers now exploring the container and their contents. Just then there was a thud and their son arrived.

"Wo xu yao chi le (I need to eat)" Xu Bo complained hungrily, "What's for dinner?"

Both parents began to giggle like children, tears rolling down their faces whilst their son looked on in complete bewilderment.

"Xia (prawns)" Li Yang finally managed to say, wiping her wet face with a sleeve.

"Lao wai xia (Foreigner prawns)" Xu Wei added, looking at his wife, "And I bet they're delicious!"

A month after starting her employment with Delia, Li Yang felt confident enough to point out where things needed to be done and the foreigner was happy for her ayi to take more responsibility, saving Delia the frustration of language barriers and getting around. Therefore, four weeks into their arrangement, Li Yang was regularly dropping off dry-cleaning, although she still couldn't understand why these people didn't wash their delicate clothing by hand like the Chinese did, paying bills at the Post Office and picking up fresh goods from the early morning market on her way to work. It wasn't a hardship for Li Yang to do these extra tasks, sometimes in fine weather she liked to pop out on various errands, and Delia had never asked her to work extra hours.

On the final day of the month however, the Friday that the ayi was due to be paid, a stumbling block came between the two women. She pressed on with her regular cleaning duties until five o'clock when it was time to leave, occasionally checking the dining table, worktops and coffee table to see if her employer had left the money out for her housekeeper. It was nowhere to be seen. Eventually, at quarter to six, after bathing her daughter, Delia walked into the kitchen and found Li Yang sipping a cup of water.

"Oh, hello," she smiled, pointing at her watch, "You should have gone home at five."

The ayi flushed a dark crimson and set down the drink, "Tai Tai Delia, today my money."

Immediately the foreign lady understood and a hand flew up to her mouth, "Oh Yang, I forgot, I'm so sorry. Wait there I'll call my husband."

In the minutes that ensued, Li Yang caught snippets of a telephone conversation between Delia and her husband. The housekeeper hadn't met the master of the house yet and wondered if he was angry at being disturbed if he was still in the office.

"My husband will bring money," Delia explained, trying to simplify her words as best as she could to make herself understood, "But he will come at seven o'clock."

Li Yang nodded, "No problem Tai Tai, I play Peggy," and trotted into the lounge to join the child.

As it happened, Ben Peel didn't arrive until almost eight, staggering through the door full of laughter and a great deal of beer, having to count out the ayi's salary twice as his eyes had become blurred from his after work drinking binge.

"Bye bye Tai Tai," Li Yang said very seriously, tucking the cash safely inside her jacket, "See you Monday."

Chapter Two

Ben & Delia Peel

"Do you think we could ask Yang to babysit Peggy while we go out for Sunday Brunch this weekend?" Ben Peel asked his wife over an early morning coffee, "It would be great to have a grown-up lunch and a few glasses of wine with some of the other expats."

"I don't see why not," Delia nodded, grabbing the last piece of buttered toast before Ben could devour it, "Peggy loves Yang and it would give me a good excuse to buy a new dress."

"Tell her we'll pay her extra of course," Ben added, "And we can leave some money for her to take Peggy to the park for ice-cream. We'd be home by six at the latest."

"Six?" repeated Delia, "I thought the brunch finished at three."

Ben gave a cheeky grin and winked, "It does, but it would be rude not to call for a couple at the Blue Sheep pub on the way home, wouldn't it?"

Later that morning Delia Peel broached the subject with her cleaning lady. She wasn't sure if the middle-aged woman would be happy to leave her own family at a weekend but friends had assured her that the Chinese were hard working and Yang would probably appreciate some extra money too.

"Yang," she smiled, carrying the kitchen calendar over to where the ayi stood cleaning the stove top, "This Sunday, could you work? No cleaning, just look after Peggy, me and my husband would like to go out."

Delia tapped the square on the calendar to show which day she meant and immediately Yang's face lit up.

"Yes, no problem," she confirmed, just as happy to be trusted with the Peel's little girl as to be earning some extra cash, "You go to eat?"

"Yes," Delia replied smugly, thinking about the champagne that would no doubt be consumed too, "We will eat and maybe have wine too."

Yang nodded and continued to clean the hob, happy that she would get to spend more time with Peggy.

"Thank you," Delia grinned excitedly and she raced off to see what she could wear to the event, although she was already planning to buy something glamorous, knowing full well that the other expat wives would be dressed up, with their hair and nails done to perfection.

As mid-week approached, Delia set off to the city centre in a taxi. She had decided to entrust Yang to care for her daughter for a couple of hours while she searched for the perfect outfit, and it would also give Peggy the chance to get used to her mother being away from home, albeit for a short duration. Stepping out onto Nanjing Dong Lu, Delia felt the full humidity of the summer heat and headed quickly for the nearest department store, standing under the air-conditioning for a few minutes before trekking off to find the women's floor.

Meanwhile, back in the apartment, Peggy sat at the kitchen table with a colouring book and crayons while Yang prepared the little girl's lunch. Delia had given instructions for her daughter to have a strawberry jam sandwich followed by a banana if she could manage it, but Peggy seemed much more interested in the shredded duck and vegetable rice that Yang had put down nearby for her own meal.

"Try," Yang urged, spooning some duck and rice into the child's mouth, "Good?"

Peggy nodded and smacked her lips together, "More."

Yang chuckled and obediently filled up the spoon again, "Ya," she told Peggy, trying to teach her the Mandarin word for duck meat, "Say ya."

"Ya," the little girl repeated, "Ya, ya, ya."

Yang put a hand affectionately upon the child's cheek, "Good girl Peggy."

The ayi was pleased to be able to feed the Peel's daughter something healthier than the sweet lunch that had been planned and watched with joy as Peggy devoured the pieces of duck with relish.

Back at the store, Delia Peel was having a nightmare. The shop assistants in the womenswear department had insisted upon following closely behind her, making extremely unsuitable suggestions on what she might like to purchase and generally being annoying. Delia was a fairly busty woman and found the attention of these flat-chested Shanghainese girls most irksome and as the temperature outside rose with the mid-day sun, so did Delia's temper. Finally, as a green taffeta number was thrust into her face, the Englishwoman turned in rage and stormed out of the shop. It took a frothy cappuccino and a pan au chocolat at a nearby French café to calm her down and, as she glanced at her watch, Delia realised that she'd been out for nearly three hours. Therefore, tired, sticky and without a dress, she hailed a taxi to take her home, feeling dishevelled and distraught. For the first time in her life Delia hated shopping.

Just as Yang had settled Peggy down for an afternoon nap, she heard the familiar sound of the front door opening and went out into the hallway expecting to see Delia laden with bags.

"Bu hao ma (Not good)?" she asked the Englishwoman, noticing her flustered face and sweating brow.

"No Yang, definitely not good," Delia gasped, heading for the kitchen and a cold glass of Chardonnay.

Yang followed and stood waiting for an explanation.

It took several minutes and a lot of unusual gestures for Delia Peel to retell the shopping trip in all its animated glory and the Chinese cleaning lady stood transfixed as she took it all in. However, at the end of the story, as Delia drained her wineglass, Yang still couldn't see where the problem lay and gave a nervous smile as she continued with her chores, leaving the Tai Tai to refill her drink.

"So why didn't she buy anything?" Xu Wei asked for the second time as Yang explained about her employer's unsuccessful trip into the city, putting in a few snippets of her own for added drama.

"Well, I don't really know," his wife confessed, "It was something to do with the shop assistants."

"We have that problem with the foreigners all the time," Xu Bo countered, looking up from his bowl of noodles, "They just won't take advice from the sales staff."

"What do you mean?" the older man asked, setting down his chopsticks and waiting for an answer.

"Well," mumbled Xu Bo, shovelling more noodles into his mouth and dripping juice down his chin, "They like to be left alone to make a decision. Apparently, it's normal for the Lao Wai to walk around by themselves trying to make a decision, and when they've made up their mind they call one of the staff over."

"But how do they know which is the best product for them?" Li Yang quizzed, filling up her son's bowl.

"That's just it," the young man told her, "They think they know best."

Not one of the family members could see the irony of Xu Bo working in an electrical store but not knowing the first thing about setting a washing- machine, programming a DVD player or putting food to cook in a microwave oven. Sales to him were simply in the form of his generated commission and naturally he always advised customers to buy the most expensive items, knowing that his own salary would reap the benefits and that he would reach his monthly sales target, regardless of not knowing what he was selling.

On Friday, things were looking bleak for Delia Peel. The entire contents of her wardrobe lay strewn across the master suite as she searched for something suitable to wear for the Sunday brunch and Yang found herself creeping around on tiptoes as the foreign woman cursed for most of the morning. By lunchtime, the Tai Tai had calmed down but still hadn't tidied up the mountain of clothes.

"I help?" Yang asked, tentatively peeping around the bedroom door, "Peggy sleeping."

Delia shrugged, her bottom lip pouting like a scorned child, "I don't know how you can help Yang."

The ayi reached for a bundle of dresses, holding them up one by one and then pulling them back onto the coat hangers, one in particular caught her eye.

"This one very, very good," she told her employer, pointing at a dark red frock. It had a scalloped neckline and flared out to just below the knee.

"Oh Yang," Delia sighed, touching the soft fabric, "It's my favourite dress but it's too tight."

"Ting bu dong (I hear but don't understand)?" Yang murmured, tilting her head slightly.

Delia pointed at her bust and waist, "Too big." Li Yang smiled, "No problem Tai Tai."

After urging Delia to put on the dress, regardless of the poor fit, Yang fetched a pair of scissors and began snipping at the seams. Delia was horrified and had tears in her eyes.

"No!" she wailed, realising what was taking place right under her nose, but Yang continued, obliviously.

"I fix," Yang stated proudly, motioning for Delia to go and take off the garment, "You see, I make ok."

Delia Peel was very unsure of what Yang proposed to do but after an hour of watching the ayi deftly remove a section of the lining and stitch it into each side to make matching panels, it was soon apparent that the Shanghainese woman was a wonderful seamstress and had transformed the tight-fitting dress with a comfortable and unnoticeable alteration.

"Oh my word," Delia squealed, "You're amazing!"

Li Yang blushed, just glad to be able to make her boss happy and now, best of all, she could set about the chore of putting away the bundles of clothes that still lay discarded around the bedroom.

"So you saved the day," Xu Wei beamed, "And also saved Mr. Peel a lot of money too. He must be very happy that his wife didn't have to buy a new dress after all."

Li Yang nodded, "These foreign women seem to put on weight much more quickly than us Chinese. They don't eat the right foods and definitely drink too much alcohol."

Her husband rubbed his head thoughtfully, "They are built very differently, that's for sure."

"We should be thankful that our race have been brought up with more sense than to eat too much chocolate and spend our evenings supping beer."

Xu Wei agreed, although on the odd occasion that he had enjoyed a Tsingtao beer with his colleagues, he'd rather enjoyed it.

Just then Xu Bo appeared, he looked flustered and tired. "Sit down son," Yang fussed, "I'll get you some iced tea."

"I'm going out in half an hour," he replied, "I just came home to get changed."

"Where?" his father enquired, raising an eyebrow. "Just to the cinema."

"Who are you going with?" Yang pushed, hoping that her son had met a young woman.

Xu Bo blushed, his pale cheeks turning pink at the question, "Just a friend."

"A female friend?" his mother called as the boy retreated to his room, "Somebody we know?"

The questions fell on deaf ears but Yang stood smiling at her husband expectantly.

"Do you think our son has finally met a girl?" she asked, "Perhaps someone from the shopping centre, a hard-working young woman perhaps?"

"Hum, I hope she has a good family," Xu Wei tutted, "Our boy has decent prospects in his job."

Yang's eyes narrowed as she thought about their only child getting married, "Maybe we should ask him to arrange a meeting between us and the girl's parents, then we can judge for ourselves."

Xu Wei snorted, it was a loud porcine noise, "At least let him go on one date first woman!"

By the time Sunday arrived, Delia Peel had made several lists of things that she needed to tell Yang about her little girl's requirements, including some instructions, and now stood, looking radiant in her newly altered red dress, going through the necessary details.

"If you go to the park, she'll need to wear a sun hat," Delia motioned, pulling a floppy bonnet from the coat rack, "And please put some of this sunblock cream on her arms and legs...."

The list went on. Yang understood some of the things that Delia was telling her but didn't feel the need to ask any questions about the instructions that she couldn't comprehend, instead convincing herself that after twenty-five years of motherhood, compared to Delia's three, she probably knew best anyway.

"Can we just go now?" Ben Peel was urging, "Or we'll be late meeting the others."

"Give mummy a big kiss," Delia told Peggy, pursing her lips and stooping down, "Be a good girl for Yang."

"Okay, bye, bye," the child giggled, waving as her parents hurried to the door.

"Ah, telephone number in case of emergencies," Delia squealed, pulling a pen and scrap of paper from her handbag, "Call me if you need to, okay, we'll come straight back?"

"Ok," Yang nodded, "Have a nice day."

As it turned out, Peggy was more than happy to spend the day with her ayi and played happily both at home and in the park.

Yang watched as the little girl waited for her turn to go on a plastic slide with a group of local children, all of them marvelling at Peggy's shiny brown curls and pale skin compared to their own straight black hair and distinct oriental features. The ayi was proud to be sitting here on the bench, knowing that the Peel's had entrusted their most precious possession to her and the bond between Yang and Peggy was growing stronger every day. The child spoke at least a dozen words of Mandarin and now proudly called 'Ni Hao' to her playmates as they mounted the ladder to the top of the slide.

A couple of hours passed before the little girl and her guardian headed home for lunch, although after a carton of orange juice and a large iced cone, it was going to be something light and cool. Yang had noticed a large tray of eggs sitting on the worktop that morning, it seemed that the dozen she'd brought from Deng Ping weren't enough for the family, so maybe that's what Peggy would like to eat, she pondered.

However, back in the apartment, cooling down under the air-conditioning, Peggy had other ideas about what she would like to eat and headed straight for the fruit bowl. Choosing the largest banana, the little girl sat happily watching her favourite cartoons while munching away. Yang headed for the kitchen to make a cup of green tea and then joined Peggy on the sofa where the pair chatted in pigeon Chinese and English until the Peel's returned home some time later.

As the front door flew open just after five o'clock, Delia Peel wobbled into the hallway, holding herself upright by pressing her palm flat against the wall. She was closely followed by her husband, who was red-faced and jolly, his short-sleeved shirt now untucked and a bit crumpled.

"Ni hao," they both called, staggering towards the living room, "Hello."

Yang sat open-mouthed. This wasn't the first time she had encountered drunken employers but she was slightly concerned that they would be looking after Peggy for the next few hours before she went to bed.

"Yang stay," she told them stiffly, "I put Peggy in bed later."

"No, no," Ben chuckled, "It's fine, you can go home now."

The man thrust some money into Yang's hand and thanked her for babysitting their daughter. Peggy thought the whole scenario hilarious and reached up for her father to take her into his arms.

"Daddy," she giggled, "Why is your hair so messy?"

"Ha, ha," came the response, "Mummy and Daddy have been out with their friends."

Right on cue, there came the clatter of shoes down the wooden hallway and four more adults entered the room, two couples, all of a similar age to the Peels.

"Hello," shouted one of the men to Peggy, "What are you watching Peggy?" The little girl scrambled back to the floor and ran to the man, "Uncle Kevin!"

During this exchange, Yang stood bewildered. She hadn't met any of the Peels friends before and encountering them for the first time whilst everyone seemed incredibly inebriated was certainly something that she really hadn't expected to happen. Still, she mused, foreigners had their ways and it seemed that Ben and Delia had very much enjoyed their day out.

"What did Peggy eat today?" Delia asked, following Yang into the kitchen as she collected her bag.

Yang recounted the food as best she could and then pointed to the eggs, "These very good and very many, but Peggy no want."

"Oh never mind," Delia smiled, stifling a hiccup as she spoke, "We'll use those later."

Yang nodded and made her way out of the home, "See you tomorrow Tai Tai."

"Ahh, she's so sweet," one of the foreign ladies laughed as the ayi put on her coat, "So lovely."

Yang tutted under her breath and let herself out, still amazed at the lifestyle of these Lao Wai.

Returning home a short while later, Yang found her husband asleep in his armchair and Xu Bo nowhere to be found. The house was tidy and something delicious simmered in a pan on the stove.

"Ah, you're back," Xu Wei murmured, stirring from his slumber, "I'll finish dinner."

Yang helped the middle-aged man to his feet, allowing him to lean on her arm as he rose, "Where's our son? Has he been working all day?"

"He came back about an hour ago," Xu Wei told her, glancing at the clock for confirmation, "But he got changed and went out again. He had his new shirt on."

Yang grinned, "So, do you think he's gone out on another date?" "It looks that way," the man confirmed, "He looked very smart."

Yang ushered her husband into the kitchen to attend to the bubbling pot, a satisfied look on her face.

"I was beginning to get worried about Xu Bo," she explained, "I was discussing his situation with Deng Ping the other day and she thinks we should go to People's Park to find him a good match."

Xu Wei rubbed his chin thoughtfully, "It's a good idea, but why don't we let our son make his own choice first? If the girl isn't from a good family we can intervene and help him to find a more suitable wife."

"We should talk to him," Yang conceded, "Soon. Let's ask him about this girl he's been dating and find out about her background. Surely we are right to be concerned about our boy?"

The couple continued to talk for a while and then sat in silence eating the chicken noodle soup that Xu Wei had so carefully prepared, each wrapped up in their own thoughts but both worried about the financial implications of an impending marriage. There would be a feast to pay for, as well as all the usual costs, and hong bao (red envelopes with money) to prepare as gifts. Although it was a heavy weight on their shoulders, the couple knew that it would be best to marry off their only child while he was still young and handsome with a secure future at the electrical store. Without the need to speak, both parents knew that they needed to work extra hours to ensure that the money pot was full.

Oblivious to their cleaning lady's worries, the Peel's continued to enjoy Sunday evening with their expat friends. With Peggy now tucked up in bed exhausted, the group turned their attention to some adult fun and started to think of some games to play, each dare more risky than the next. It wasn't to be until the following morning that Yang, and the rest of the gated community, would find out exactly what had occurred at Apartment 301 that night.

Li Yang was slightly later than usual setting off that Monday morning, having stayed up late to question her son as he sneaked back in just past midnight. Although the conversation had been brief, Yang could see that Xu Bo had something to hide by his glowing red-face on finding his mother still awake. She had gently tried to cajole the information out of him by offering to make her son a warm drink but had ended up pressing him a little too hard as he fought to keep his private life under wraps. Xu Bo would never disrespect his parents by telling them to keep their noses out of his private life but neither was he willing to freely explain who, or what, had kept him out so late and the brief interlude ended in a stalemate on both sides.

Riding steadily along the busy lanes on her electric scooter, Yang now replayed her son's words in her mind and was convinced that he had something to hide. However, getting to the bottom of it might be harder than she had firstly anticipated, and she must use a degree of tact and ingenuity, she thought. Swerving suddenly to avoid a stray dog, the ayi slowed down and turned her thoughts towards Peggy. She wondered if all foreign children were used to seeing their parents drunk. For her own part, she could recollect her father taking alcohol on just a few occasions, mainly Chinese New Year celebrations when uncles and aunts would all descend upon the family home, and once at a cousin's wedding when a distant relative had brought four bottles of Mao Tai to share. She shook her head in remembrance, what a day!

As Li Yang parked up and set about locking her moped, she was suddenly approached by a security guard.

"Ni hao," he greeted, waving a white envelope in his hand, "Can you take this to your employer?"

The woman tilted her head slightly to avoid the glare from the morning son and looked curiously at the uniformed guard, "Yes, what is it?"

"Something official from the management office," he cautioned, "There was some trouble here last night, quite a mess I believe. I've only just come on duty so I don't know the full details."

Yang secured the lock on her scooter and carefully took the envelope with both hands, it wasn't sealed and she could see the stamp of the complex manager in bold red ink.

"Mei wen ti," she said softly, "No problem," although alarm bells were ringing inside her head.

Stepping into the lift of the Peel's building, the ayi pressed the button for the third floor and looked at herself in the full-length mirror that covered one side of the cubicle. An honest face looked back but she couldn't help the curiosity that was welling up inside and quickly slid the folded letter out of its envelope and scanned the contents with her eyes. As she began to read, Yang's jaw fell open but she composed herself as the automatic doors slid open and popped the letter into the pocket of her anorak.

Inside Apartment 301, Delia Peel was preparing coffee and looked a bit worse for wear.

"Morning Tai Tai," Yang called as she breezed through the door, her mind still racing, "I do that."

She took the coffee pot from Delia's grasp and pulled out one of the tubular kitchen chairs for her employer to sit on. Delia feigned a smile and put her head in hands, nursing her hangover.

"Tai Tai," Yang ventured as she poured boiling water onto ground coffee, "Yesterday..."

Delia peeked one eye out through her fingers and blinked at the ayi, "Yes, what about it?"

It was difficult for the Chinese woman to find sufficient English words to make her employer understand, so she gave a sigh and padded over to the counter where they usually kept the tray of eggs.

"Eggs finished," she said slowly, pointing to the empty space.

Delia groaned and nodded her head, careful not to move too much as it still throbbed terribly.

"Yes, all finished Yang."

"Na li ma," Yang questioned, "Where?"

She could see the Englishwoman flinching slightly at the recollection of the night before but stood awaiting a response.

"We drank too much pi jao, beer," Delia confessed, unsure why she felt the need to explain her actions to the cleaning lady, "And then we played a joke."

Li Yang frowned, she didn't understand.

Delia pulled her dressing-gown tightly around her middle and pointed at the balcony that ran along the outside of the utility room, "We throw eggs, down there, hit people with them."

Yang peered down to the ground floor. What Mrs. Peel was telling her sounded pretty much the same as the management company had stated in their letter, it seemed that the Lao Wei and their friends had been having an egg fight with passers-by, seeing who could hit their target.

"Bu hao, very bad," Li Yang muttered to herself, but it was too late and her employer heard the words as soon as they were spoken. She flushed red in embarrassment.

"Too much drinking," Delia groaned, reaching for the coffee pot, "I am so, so sorry."

The ayi pretended to fold a tea towel as she decided what to do. She liked working for the Peel's and she was certainly smitten with Peggy, it would be a shame if they had to leave the complex but the official letter had given her the impression that the foreigners behaviour would not be tolerated.

She spent the rest of the day thinking and cleaning, only stopping for a brief lunch and two cups of green tea.

By mid-afternoon, Delia Peel was feeling back to her old self again and ventured out for a walk with Peggy. However, on their return home she was feeling rather self-conscious from all the strange looks being given by local residents, indicating that they all knew about her antics from the night before. It may be best to lie low for a while, she told herself, or perhaps move altogether. Delia felt mortified that an idyllic afternoon had turned into a drunken fiasco. Although, she contemplated, it had actually been her who had thrown the first egg, hitting one of the security guards on the back of the head and knocking his hat off. Oh, how her friends had laughed. The look on the guards face had been one of the funniest sights they'd seen for ages, still, here in the cold light of day she could see why not everyone had seen the humorous side of their daring game.

At five o'clock, Li Yang took off her work apron and slipped her arms into her pink anorak. She had one last thing to do before returning home and hoped that she wasn't too late.

Gu Luo sat upright behind his mahogany desk, looking the middle-aged woman up and down.

"So, this is a custom you say?" he grunted, lighting a cigarette and puffing steadily.

"Yes," Li Yang lied, terrified that something in her demeanour would cause the official to question her further, "It's to celebrate the end of Spring."

"But we are already one month into the Summer," the rotund man countered, flicking ash into a small porcelain bowl, "How can this be so?"

"These foreigners," the ayi told him, "They do things differently and have strange lunar cycles in their calendar year, not at all like ours."

"But still," Gu Luo contemplated, making a ring of smoke as he puffed and snorted, "Throwing eggs at people is unacceptable. Officer Mo could have been seriously injured."

"It won't happen again," Li Yang promised, "Mr and Mrs. Peel have seen the error in their judgement and have asked me to send you their sincere apologies. They are both very sorry."

Mr. Gu smoothed the buttons on his tightly fitting suit and stubbed out the cigarette, rising to open the door for the woman as he did so, "Very well, we shall let it go this time, but please convey to your employers that they must behave according to our Chinese culture in the future."

Li Yang nodded and stepped out of the smoky office, stifling a cough. Once outside, she turned to bid the site manager farewell.

"Thank you, Mr. Gu," she said sincerely, "I will try my best to show these Lao Wei how to abide by our Chinese regulations. I'm sure they will understand."

The pompous man nodded in approval and returned to his desk. Whatever next, he thought to himself, who had ever heard of the 'Egg-Throwing Festival'?

Chapter Three

Chuck Rosenberry

Snapping the phone back down into its cradle, Li Yang smiled contentedly. The Ayi Agency had just assigned her to another job. It was only Saturdays, but the work wasn't strenuous and the extra money would make a difference to her regular income. Folding up the scrap of paper on which she'd written the address of her new assignment, she rolled her new employer's name off her tongue trying, with considerable difficulty, to pronounce the 'R' in his surname.

"Lo - zen - be- li," she attempted, wondering if the American would mind her calling him just 'Mister.'

These foreigners had such long and strange family names, she mused, putting on her coat and setting off for the Peel's apartment. Oh well, as long as he let her get on with the housework in peace, everything would be fine. Only two more days and Yang would find out whom she was going to be working for. An occasion hadn't yet arisen where Delia Peel had asked Li Yang to babysit Peggy on a Saturday and she hoped that it wouldn't happen, as some employers were funny about their ayis working two jobs. For now, at least, she wouldn't mention Mr. Rosenberry but would hope that things worked themselves out.

On Saturday morning, with a clean apron and her lunch tucked securely into her bag, Li Yang set off down the back lanes on her scooter, taking in the morning sun and fresh breeze. She was oblivious to the rotting vegetables and litter piled up at the side of the road, the result of yesterday's market stalls lining the roads, as this was a weekly occurrence and soon a team of local government employees would be out sweeping the streets and clearing up the mess. The heat was already intense for an early May morning and the Shanghainese woman wished that she hadn't bothered to put on her pink anorak after all. Traffic was busy and as she passed the subway station, a long line of taxis waited to pick up a fare. It was rare that Li Yang and Xu Wei had occasion to spend their money on such a luxury as a taxi and she pondered at the youngsters now jumping in, to be taken here or there, uncaring of the cost that such a luxury would set them back. She knew that Xu Bo sometimes took a cab with his friends as she had observed him coming home late out of the bedroom window, the illuminated taxi light glowing in the darkened street.

Ten minutes ride later, Li Yang arrived at the high-rise block of flats that housed Mr. Rosenberry.

"Good Morning Li Yang," a slightly built American in his early forties, with thinning hair and watery blue eyes, greeted her at the door, "Nice to meet you. Come on in."

He was wearing a faded black t-shirt and a pair of cotton shorts bearing a sports slogan.

"Good Morning," the ayi returned, flushing slightly on seeing the man's bare legs, "Mister...."

"Oh just call me Chuck," the man replied, grinning widely to show perfectly straight white teeth, "If you tell me what you need, I can give you the money to go get it."

Yang gave Mr. Rosenberry a puzzled look and followed him into the kitchen.

"Na li..." she began, "Where..."

The American opened a cupboard underneath the sink, revealing two cloths and a bottle of household cleaning spray, "This is it I'm afraid Yang, I have no idea what you might need."

Li Yang padded out to the tiny balcony where she expected to find a mop and bucket, but there was nothing apart from a clothes airer on a pulley above her head. She took a deep breath, searching for the words in English to explain that she would need to purchase some items but, turning around, Chuck was already opening a brown leather wallet and taking out some Renminbi.

"You buy?" he asked, handing the Chinese woman three red notes, "Sorry."

Li Yang nodded and took the cash, counting it carefully before slipping it into her pocket, "No problem."

After a slow start to her first day, Yang returned to Chuck Rosenberry's apartment laden with cleaning products, a broom, mop and bucket and a feather duster. She hadn't yet been given a key and had to juggle the purchases whilst buzzing the security intercom, wait to be admitted, carry everything into the lift unaided and then knock once again on the door of her employer's home. Given the exertion of her task and city heat, the ayi was already feeling slightly exhausted, beads of sweat trickling down her back.

It was a full five minutes before the American opened the door and admitted his cleaning lady. At least by this time he was dressed in a pair of beige chinos and a loosely fitting white shirt, however, avoiding any further embarrassment on Yang's part. That much she was grateful for.

"I'm going to go out now," Mr. Rosenberry said slowly in his thick Texan drawl, "see you later."

Li Yang nodded silently and watched him close the door. She looked around at the empty apartment, which was small and lacked a woman's touch. There were a lot of CD's and DVD's on display, she noticed, but no family photos or signs that Chuck Rosenberry had a wife. Several scenarios played through Yang's mind, wondering why this middle-aged man was still single, if indeed, he really was.

She began her duties in the kitchen, firstly opening up the small refrigerator to put away a carton of milk that Chuck had left on the side. Li Yang couldn't help but notice how sparse the shelves were, containing only a few bottles of beer, some cheese and a block of butter. No wonder Mr. Rosenberry is so slim, she thought to herself, he lacks someone to cook for him. What a pity!

Moving gradually around the apartment, the ayi scrubbed, dusted and mopped, stopping only to eat her lunch and take a glass of water. She had decided to leave the bedroom until the afternoon as, in her experience, it would be the room which needed the most attention. In this case she was right.

Chuck Rosenberry's bedroom was a complete disgrace.

There was an ashtray on the bedside table brimming with cigarette butts, clothes littered all over the floor and an empty pizza box lying open on the bed, the remains of some thick crusts gone hard and some congealed mayonnaise. Yang wrinkled up her nose as she carried the take-away remains to the bin, noticing that the pizza had been extra-large, too big for just one person to consume. She returned to the bedroom and set about changing the sheets, which looked as though they had been used for well over a month without washing. It didn't take long to find clean linen but in doing so, Yang discovered a box tied with a wide length of ribbon. She was tempted to look inside, but on second thoughts wasn't confident that she could re-tie the bow in the exact same way that she now found it.

At four o'clock Chuck Rosenberry returned and gave the apartment a fleeting glance before paying Yang her salary for the day and thanking her very much.

"Looks great, Yang," he grinned, "Excellent job."

Li Yang flinched as she caught the smell of beer on her employer's breath, although it was faint and couldn't have been from the consumption of more than a couple of glasses.

"I wash sheets," she told him, pointing at the automatic washing-machine. The American's cheeks reddened, "Aww, shucks, you didn't need to…."

"Very dirty," Li Yang told him, unashamed at her own boldness, "Every week I do."

Chuck nodded, understanding how things were going to be if he were to keep Li Yang as his ayi. She seemed a headstrong woman, but the apartment looked great and he could always go out while she cleaned to avoid any unnecessary chastisement. The pair eyed each other for a split second and then Yang left, satisfied that she had the upper hand.

As the weeks passed, and the temperature soared, Li Yang fell into a steady routine, working for the Peel household from Monday to Friday and cleaning for Chuck Rosenberry every Saturday. Admittedly, she was feeling tired and most of her own household chores now had to be borne by Xu Wei, but he didn't grumble. In the grand scheme of things, the extra money was being set aside for Xu Bo's impending marriage, an event which both parents looked forward to with great relish.

"Wife, put up your feet," Xu Wei ordered one evening, "And tell me about your day."

Li Yang shrugged, "Well, as it's Saturday, I went to Mr. Chuck's apartment. It wasn't too bad, but I have to confess that I fell asleep on the sofa for an hour while he was out. Hence this afternoon I had to run around like crazy to get everything done."

Xu Wei eyed his beloved and shook his head, "Bu hao," he grunted, "Very bad."

"Husband, it's so hot and I'm not as young as I used to be," Yang confided, "We need the extra money."

Xu Wei stood pondering. He wondered if there was an alternative way to earn some extra cash without Li Yang having to work so many hours. At present he couldn't think of anything and settled back in his chair, a wave of tiredness now washing over him as he watched his wife drift into a peaceful nap.

The following week, Yang arrived at Mr. Rosenberry's apartment an hour before her usual time. Having been invited to eat with her neighbours that very evening, she hadn't told him in advance, as they had no means of communication by phone, with her little English and his non-existent Mandarin, but she was sure it wouldn't be a problem. As the Sun family wanted her and Xu Wei to dine with them at six, an early start would give her chance to go home and change clothes before arriving at the neighbour's home.

"Ni hao," Yang called, pressing the apartment intercom for the second time, "Mr. Chuck, it's Yang."

The security door buzzed and she let herself in, although on reaching her workplace, Yang had to wait another few minutes before Chuck opened the door, looking extremely flustered.

"Ah, you're early," the American stated, "I'm still in bed."

Yang looked the skinny man up and down. His hair was messed up and a towel was wrapped around his tiny waist to cover up his modesty. His hairless top half was bare and it embarrassed her.

"No problem," she told him firmly and pushed past to the kitchen, leaving Chuck open-mouthed.

As Li Yang opened the fridge to put her lunch inside, she heard voices in the bedroom.

"Sssshhh," Chuck Rosenberry was whispering, "You need to go."

There was a deep-throated giggle and then the sound of water running in the bathroom.

Yang flushed slightly. She hadn't expected Chuck to have a visitor and they had clearly shared a bed the night before. She pulled out some cleaning rags and set to work in the living room, keeping a steady eye on the bedroom door while she worked. Occasionally there would be a muffled conversation but mostly just the sounds of people moving around on the other side of the wall, doing goodness knows what.

After half an hour, Chuck Rosenberry emerged, dressed in shorts, t-shirt and tennis shoes. Li Yang looked up expectantly as if waiting for him to strike up a conversation.

"I'll give you your money now," he said, shuffling across the room, the laces on his footwear hanging loose as he walked, "I might not be back until later."

Li Yang blinked, not understanding but took her wages gladly.

"Yang have key?" she asked, thinking it only natural in case she needed to go out on an errand.

The American pretended not to hear and backed out down the hallway, ushering his friend outside before the ayi could catch a glimpse, his laces still flicking from side to side as he trotted along behind the girl.

However, Yang was incredibly intrigued and set down her tools before racing over to the window, which she opened just enough to peer down. A rush of hot air hit her face, momentarily steaming up her glasses, and during the process of clearing them she almost missed the object of her curiosity. Holding on to the ledge, she craned her neck, trying to see who or what Chuck was ushering into a taxi just outside the gate. There was a pair of very long legs, tanned and shapely, a red skirt that was far too short to belong to a woman of good intentions, beautiful thick black hair, unmistakably Asian, and long red fingernails adorned with rings that sparkled in the morning sunshine. She looked a real beauty.

Li Yang pulled her head back inside and closed the window. Now she knew that Chuck Rosenberry had a girlfriend, although it was beyond her what a middle-aged American and a very young Asian woman would have to talk about. Just wait until she told Xu Wei!

Continuing her chores, the ayi pondered if this was the reason that she wasn't given a key to the door, perhaps her employer was trying to keep his love life a secret.

That evening, after dining with the Sun's, Li Yang and Xu Wei went back to their tiny home and sat talking in the kitchen. Yang was annoyed that Xu Bo hadn't joined them and her husband was trying to placate her.

"It's fine," he soothed, "Xu Bo doesn't want to listen to us old people chatting."

"It's impolite," retorted Yang, placing a hand on her heart and sighing, "I must tell him to buy a small gift for Mrs. Sun by way of apology. Xu Bo is testing my patience these days."

Xu Wei nodded, "Yes, I agree. It's not a good way to behave. Where is he anyway?"

Li Yang got up and went to stand by the window as if her son would appear if she did so. There were hundreds of people milling about on the streets and in the nearby park, all trying to cool down now that the evening breeze had arrived. Xu Bo was not one of them.

"Ren shan, ren hai," she told her husband, "People mountain, people sea."

Xu Wei simpered at the Chinese proverb. It had been a long time since he'd heard that particular phrase, denoting that the city of Shanghai was filled with citizens everywhere you cared to look.

"Sit down," he told Yang, "Xu Bo will be home soon enough and then we can question him."

But Xu Bo didn't come home that night, neither did he call or answer his parents repeated text messages.

The following day, the couple contacted Xu Bo's work friends, who assured them that he was fine and staying with a new acquaintance on the other side of the city. They tried to take their minds off their only child by taking a walk and watching television, but silently each was tormented, wondering what on earth Xu Bo was up to and how the situation could be rectified.

At midnight on Sunday the couple eventually rose and retired to their bed. Li Yang tried to fight the onset of slumber but she was exhausted and soon drifted into a hazy dream of foreigners, Chinese girls and Mrs. Sun's excellent cooking. It wasn't until the door-latch clicked shut that she stirred, sleepily reaching for the bedside clock and nudging her husband to wake up.

"Go back to sleep," Xu Wei whispered, rubbing his wife's arm, "It's still early."

"Is that Xu Bo?" she enquired, fluttering her eyes, "It's five o'clock in the morning!"

"Sshhh, we can talk to him later," the man at her side murmured, "Not now."

But it was too late. Li Yang was now wide awake and curious as to where their son had been all night and, more importantly, who he had been keeping company with.

"Xu Bo," she called, making her way down the hall, "Where have you been?"

"Not now mother," came a low voice, "I am too tired to talk, let me sleep."

At seven o'clock, as Xu Wei left the apartment, he knocked heavily on his son's bedroom door.

"Get up Xu Bo," he implored, "You need to eat breakfast before you go to work."

Silence.

"Xu Wei," fussed Li Yang, ushering her husband out through the front door, "Leave it to me, I'll make sure he gets up before I leave. Go now or you'll be late."

The man reluctantly turned to go, sighing heavily as he stared at the closed bedroom door.

"See you tonight," he muttered.

As soon as the door had closed, Li Yang called to her son, "Xu Bo, are you awake?"

There was not so much as a murmur inside and the woman entered the room.

Xu Bo was hidden underneath a cotton sheet, his body curled up and his head under the pillow.

"You must get up now," his mother scolded, "You have to be at the store in less than an hour."

As she waited for a response, Yang scanned the room. Everything was in its place except for a white shirt that hung on the bedpost. She picked it up and held it up to look properly. This looked like a brand new shirt, and it smelled distinctly of perfume. She held it up looking for any tell-tale marks.

"Xu Bo!" she said sharply, raising her voice, "Wake up! Where have you been all night?"

The young man stirred slightly, but only a foot slid from beneath its cotton shroud.

"Mother, I'm not well," Xu Bo pleaded, "Please leave me in peace. We can talk later."

Yang stood wringing her hands, wondering if her son was telling the truth, it was certainly unlike him to miss a day's work. She would give him the benefit of the doubt just for today.

"I'll phone your manager," she sighed after a thirty second pause, deciding what to do, "You rest."

Xo Bo rolled over and resumed his slumber, a satisfied smile spreading across his face as he slept.

Within ten minutes, the young man's mother had managed to convince the electrical store manager that her son was genuinely sick and then collected her own lunch to take to work. Little did Li Yang know that her son was simply shattered from a night on the Shanghai tiles, so to speak.

Throughout the day, Yang pulled out her telephone and sent a text message to Xu Bo, checking to see if he felt better, but she received no reply and spent a good deal of time worrying about her child.

"Is everything okay Yang?" Delia Peel asked, noticing that her ayi had been cleaning the same mirror for almost ten minutes.

"Yes tai tai, sorry," Yang replied, suddenly realising that she was being spoken to, "No problem."

Delia didn't want to pry, besides she lacked the Mandarin language skills to enquire further, but she could see that the Chinese woman wasn't her usual relaxed self.

"Go home early Yang," Delia told her cleaning lady, "You look tired. I'll see you tomorrow."

It was only two o'clock, but despite feeling guilty at drawing her employer's eye to her lack of attention, Yang wanted nothing more than to return home to check on Xu Bo.

"Thank you," she sighed, picking up her bag and jacket from the hallway, "See you tomorrow."

Delia Peel watched the little woman disappear and wondered what had happened to cause such a change in the ayi's demeanour. It was very unlike Yang to be stressed about anything.

Back at Li Yang's apartment, Xu Bo was unaware of his mother's early return and stood in the kitchen, snacking on potato crisps and chocolate that he'd just been out to buy from the local shop. The radio was tuned to a station playing pop music and a men's fashion magazine lay open on the table.

With the distraction of the magazine, noise from the radio and enjoyment of his treats, Xu Bo didn't hear the front door latch and was caught completely by surprise as his bewildered mother tottered in.

"Oi Yor," Li Yang exclaimed, looking at the scene before her, "What's going on?"

"Er," Xu Bo started, his eyes as wide as a rabbit caught in headlights, "Mother, I wasn't expecting you back until much later."

"I can see that," Yang tutted, reaching over to switch off the music, "What's got into you these days?!"

"Nothing," the young man whined, rapidly pulling the magazine out of sight, "I didn't feel well earlier."

Li Yang waved a hand and rubbed her temples, "Xu Bo, leave me. I can't talk to you now."

And so, the task of giving their son a good talking to about his recent behaviour, fell upon Xu Wei that very evening. From her seat in the living room, Li Yang could hear a heated discussion in the kitchen but kept clear of the source, hoping instead that her husband could sort out this terrible situation. Neither

parent could understand why Xu Bo was suddenly going out and not returning home at night, but both believed quite sincerely that any young woman
who was allowing herself to be courted in such a way was both immoral and
unsuitable as a wife for their son. Something would have to be done.

Xu Wei hadn't seemed to extract many answers from his son, however, and
a heavy silence fell upon the family over the next few days, each in their own
personal turmoil about the situation and each determined to find their own
solution. Xu Bo, however, had no intention of revealing anything to his parents.

By Saturday morning, things had calmed slightly and Li Yang set off to Chuck
Rosenberry's home feeling slightly better than in recent days.

Although the true source of Xu Bo's uncharacteristic behaviour still remained a mystery, the tense atmosphere had cleared slightly and Xu Bo was
now back at work.

As usual, Li Yang rang the buzzer and waited to be allowed in.

"Morning Yang," the American smiled, opening the door wide, "It's going to
be a scorcher today."

"Sorry I…." Yang began, confused by the man's terminology of the weather.
"Very hot Yang," Chuck explained, unusually cheerful for the early hour.

"Yes," she nodded, realising that indeed the sun was blazing today, "Very hot."

As the Texan backed away, grabbing his bedroom door handle in the process, Li Yang felt the familiar seed of curiosity plant itself firmly in her mind.
Mr. Rosenberry undoubtedly had his lady friend in there she thought, keeping
her hidden from the ayi's prying eyes.

As she began work, Li Yang wondered if her own son could possibly be
spending his nights with one of these 'loose' Asian girls. Surely not, she mused,
such a relationship would bring nothing but shame and embarrassment to her
family. Xu Bo was probably just enjoying the Shanghai music scene.

Just as Yang began sweeping the corridor, Chuck opened the bedroom door
and peered out.

"Ah Yang," he laughed nervously, "I'm going out soon."

"Okay," Li Yang nodded, continuing to sweep the floor, "No problem."

The slight American leaned against the doorpost nervously watching his
cleaning lady at her task.

"I, er, have a friend here," he chortled, wondering if an explanation of the
woman inside his bedroom was entirely necessary, "We will go out together."

Li Yang shrugged, suddenly becoming aware that her employer was hoping to discreetly exit the property with his overnight guest unseen by the ayi.

"Yang finish soon," the cleaner replied steadily, fixing her eye upon the room behind Chuck.

"Ok, good," he grinned, retreating slightly, "Thank you."

The bedroom door closed leaving the ayi intrigued and red-faced.

Li Yang moved her basket of cleaning products and hefty broom into the living room a few minutes later, but continued to focus her full attention on the bedroom door which was still within sight.

There were muffled voices but the English being spoken was too quick and without pause for her to comprehend. It sounded as though the couple were having a disagreement of some kind.

Yang plumped up cushions and straightened the chairs, trying to pull her inquisitive thoughts away from the foreign man and his guest. It really wasn't any of her business what Chuck Rosenberry got up to in his nocturnal pursuits but she really couldn't fathom the cloak and dagger charades.

As the ayi moved across to the chair, something red and leathery caught her eye. It was nestled tightly between the seat pad and the chair, having obviously become wedged between the two. Yang pushed her fingers down the side of the space and pulled. The first attempt only succeeded in pushing the object further down into the gap but a second, firmer grasp brought the item free. It was a large purse. However, unfortunately it was the kind that clip together at the top and the erratic movement of freeing it had caused the clip to open, showering credit cards, bus tickets and coins onto the chair.

Li Yang hurriedly gathered up the scattered things, rapidly stuffing them back into the purse as fast as she could, terrified that her employer would think she'd been rifling through the other woman's personal effects. She listened hard for any sign that the bedroom occupants were about to leave but felt satisfied that she had time to put the purse contents back in order before anyone was the wiser.

Then Yang stopped. Her fingers had struck upon an identity card, a simple plastic outer with photograph of the young woman whom she presumed was now here in the apartment. She was beautiful. Li Yang guessed that the woman was around twenty five years old, and new to Shanghai too, by the date stamped on the permit. Brown doleful eyes gazed at the ayi from the snapshot, with long dark lashes and a slender neck. Yang brushed a finger over the photograph and sighed, what a lovely young woman. But there was something not quite right, she couldn't say what, but it troubled Yang immensely.

She glanced down at the country of origin and managed to make out the word 'Philippines'. So that's why the woman hadn't looked like a typical Shanghainese girl, Yang realised. But still, there was more, although unable to understand any of the other information on the card, she quickly scanned her eyes over the lettering and pushed it into the purse, closing the top firmly.

"Yang," called Chuck Rosenberry, sidling out of the bedroom and ushering his long-legged friend down the hallway, "We'll be going now."

"Mr. Chuck," the ayi replied, rushing forward to where he stood ready to make a quick escape, "This in chair. Yang find."

She handed over the red leather purse, hoping that her own flushed cheeks wouldn't relay the fact that she'd looked at the contents.

"Oh, thanks!" the Texan smiled, and then turning to his lover, "Roxy, you nearly forgot this."

Catching a glimpse of the retreating Filipino woman, clad once again in high heels and short skirt, Li Yang shyly raised a hand to acknowledge that the visitor had been seen.

"Bye bye," she told the beauty, "See you again."

With a flip of the hair and a wink, the stunning lady was gone, with her American lover following eagerly behind. All that could be heard as the couple left was the click clacking of heels on the tiled floor outside.

It wasn't until a couple of hours later, as she cleaned the bathroom, that Li Yang had a revelation.

There, on the side of the white enamel sink, was a bottle of pills. She knew that the medicine was on prescription as it was easy to recognise the familiar brown pharmaceutical plastic container, printed on the front with the patients full details.

Yang squinted, without her glasses it was difficult to read the tiny print. "Chuck Rosenberry, Date of birth 12.05.50, Sex Male."

There was nothing incredible about the words printed there and it was near impossible for Li Yang to read out the name of the prescription pills, let alone understand what they were. But something made her stop. She recognised a word in English that she had seen only a few hours before.

"Male," she repeated, turning the bottle over in her hand to look again, "It says male."

As the implications of the word suddenly dawned on Li Yang she grasped the side of the bathtub and sat down, shaking slightly as she did so.

The word 'Male' had also appeared on the Filipino 'woman's' identity card!

"Oh my word," the cleaning lady sighed, breathing slowly in and out to calm her growing fears, "Mr. Chuck's been having one of those lady boy people over to stay!"

Li Yang replaced the pills on the side of the sink, her fingers still unsteady as her mind raced.

"Yang go home," she told herself, rushing down the corridor to put on her anorak, "No, Yang wait for Mr. Chuck to pay money, then Yang go home but not come back."

Li Yang sat down to wait, determined that her work for Chuck Rosenberry was well and truly over.

Chapter Four

Frau Henckel

In the leafy suburbs of Pudong, far beyond the reaches of the inner city ring roads of Shanghai's bursting metropolis, stands a vast housing complex where white brick mansions sit side by side in tranquil harmony. Inside their vast interiors, you will find sweeping staircases, crystal chandeliers and marble bathrooms. Inside these immense homes of grandeur and luxury, you could be almost anywhere in the world, where it not for the bustling Chinese staff who rush to and fro serving their master's every whim.

Shanghai's growing millionaires and entrepreneurs live here, alongside company directors from every corner of the globe, each oblivious to the other's existence, save for the occasional nod of the head in acknowledgment as they come and go about their daily business.

Chauffeurs, maids, cooks and gardeners tarry back and forth every day, earning their living by doing a hard day's labour in this almost fairy tale world. Never in their lifetime can the workers imagine a life so full of opulence and ease to which their employers are accustomed but neither to they crave this life where it seems that everything is taken for granted but nothing is ever enough.

It was to one of these sprawling residences that Xu Wei now rode his electric scooter, enjoying the breeze on his face as he travelled wide-eyed and expectant towards his very first part-time job. Despite toiling long hours at the factory all week, the desire to earn funds towards his son's future had taken on a more urgent importance in recent weeks and now that Li Yang had refused to return to her Saturday work with Chuck Rosenberry, the Chinese man had taken it upon himself to find work as a gardener for one day every week.

Counting the numbers on the heavy brass-plates as he rode past each house, Xu Wei came to an abrupt halt outside number seventy-three and eyed the immaculate façade for a moment before locking up his scooter and rushing up the front steps. He stood for just a few seconds before the door was opened by a Shanghainese woman of around thirty years old, wearing a starched blue uniform and white pumps.

"Ni hao," she greeted Xu Wei, staring unblinking at the man, "What can I do for you?"

"I'm here to work," he explained, lifting his bag of tools to show the maid, "To do the garden."

"Oi Yor!" the woman exclaimed, pulling a face, "Go around the back! Never use this entrance!"

The front door was immediately closed, leaving Xu Wei slightly bewildered before he realised that his etiquette was in error and of course a worker should use the tradesman's entrance in such a place.

The maid was already waiting expectantly by the time Xu Wei had sauntered around to the rear of the mansion, taking in the vast garden as he went, and in her hand she held a key.

"The mistress said that everything you will need is in the garage," she instructed, "You use this."

Xu Wei took the key and nodded, "Mei wen ti, no problem."

The woman looked the new gardener up and down before retreating inside and closing the door.

As Xu Wei unlocked stood looking at the grounds, he realised that his own meagre equipment, consisting of pruners, shears and a trowel, would be no match for the task at hand. The garden was huge, spreading out around the back of the property and disappearing down a grassy slope some way in the distance. There were willow trees, magnolia, cherry blossom and apple trees, settled amongst hydrangea bushes and wild bamboo. It would certainly keep him occupied for some weeks ahead.

Unlocking the garage to peruse his new employer's gardening equipment, Xu Wei switched on the electric light and gazed in awe at the sight before his eyes. A luxurious black car took up half of the garage space, its shiny metallic body glistening against the overhead strip lights. Never before had the man seen such a vehicle up close. Xu Wei peered inside, his own reflection looking back at him through blacked out glass, unable to see anything of the car's magnificent interior.

There was a cough behind him, forcing Xu Wei to turn, startled and alarmed.

"Ni hao," the person said in clipped Mandarin, with just the slightest hint of a foreign accent, "Xu Wei?"

"Dui, Xu Wei," he managed, facing the speaker and confirming that he was indeed whom the foreigner thought he was, "Wo gong si, I'm here to work."

The person nodded and smiled like a cat, smugly and knowingly, but Xu Wei was still unable to distinguish whether he was in the presence of a male or female.

"Frau Henckel," the foreigner offered, putting out a hand, expecting Xu Wei to shake it.

He did so limply, confused by the title and in awe of the muscular frame of his new employer but desperately trying to maintain a semblance of composure on his first day here.

"The tools are there," the person confirmed, pointing to a large rack, "See you later."

Setting to work, raking leaves to begin with, while he decided how and where to tackle first in the garden area, Xu Wei pondered his first encounter with Frau Henckel. His confusion was forefront. The person to whom he had spoken when applying for this position had stated that it would be a woman to whom Xu Wei would report, but there was very little to distinguish the person whom he had met as female in gender. Her dark hair was cropped short, right back over her ears, with the top being combed smooth with wax or gel and nothing in the woman's posture had given a hint of her femininity. Frau Henckel had been dressed in a dark pin-striped suit, with a white shirt underneath, buttoned right up to the neck and, although the meeting had been brief, Xu Wei hadn't been able to make out the shape of a bust or waistline.

Still, there was little time to dwell on such thoughts, as he tackled the prickly overgrown rose bushes and attempted to tame the tall shafts of bamboo. It was only as Xu Wei took a well-deserved break that he turned his attention to the person indoors, feeling a pair of eyes watching him from somewhere upstairs.

There it was again, the fleeting glimpse of a tall shadow, peering at him from behind the curtains, drawing back quickly as soon as he allowed his eyes to travel upwards. Xu Wei straightened and got to his feet, it was already mid-afternoon and there were still many unattended tasks that he wished to attend to before leaving for the day.

"Ah, there you are finally," Li Yang sighed, coming into the tiny hallway to greet her husband, "Let me take your jacket, here put on your slippers and come into the kitchen, dinner will be ready soon."

Xu Wei laughed, "Stop fussing wife, all this because I've done a day's work!"

"An extra day's work," Yang reminded him, "You are such a good husband."

"And a hungry one!" added Xu Wei, shuffling into the kitchen, "It's been a very busy day."

"The lao wei?" his wife questioned, wanting to know all about the foreign employer, "Is he or she okay?"

Xu Wei crumpled up his face, not quite knowing how to explain, he didn't know whether Li Yang would understand what he had to report and decided to keep his explanation for another day.

"Hen hao," he finally settled upon, "Very good. But the garden is very big, I have plenty to keep me busy."

Li Yang smiled, happy that they would once again have some extra cash going into Xu Bo's wedding pot, although judging by their son's noticeable absence, another talk on the subject was impending.

By the second Saturday of Xu Wei's new employment, he felt more confident at being allowed to make decisions regarding the upkeep of the mansion gardens. It had been many years since he'd helped his uncle to attend to the grounds on the family farm and, although this new position could hardly be compared to that of his youth, Xu Wei was enjoying the challenge of putting the place in order. Nobody had asked about his competency or experience as a gardener, but he felt sure that with just a little common sense, most horticultural problems could be resolved. He was also finding the ride out to the suburbs pleasurable as he seldom had opportunity to ride his moped out of the city limits and this new venture provided both thinking time and an interesting landscape.

"Ah, Xu Wei," Frau Henckel purred, striding across the lawn in soft leather loafers, this time wearing a skirt, her hands clasped firmly behind her back, "Zen me ban (What's to be done now)?"

Xu Wei put down the hoe that he'd been using to weed the borders and put up a hand to shield his eyes from the mid-day sun, shocked to discover that his employer was actually a woman, as he explained his plan to spruce up the grounds. He looked sideways at the solid frame and broad shoulders beside him.

Frau Henckel nodded her approval, able to comprehend the name of each plant, much to the gardener's admiration as he pointed at the different areas and shrubs.

"Xie xie (thank you)," she finally offered, turning to leave, "Hen hao Xu Wei."

The man glowed with pride, delighted that his efforts were being noticed, and watched the tall manly female return to the house, pausing only to wipe her shoes on the doormat as she entered.

"Xu Wei," a woman called an hour later, "Tai tai has something for you."

Dropping his tools and crossing the grass, Xu Wei headed expectantly for the kitchen door.

"Here," the maid told him, handing the gardener a plastic bag, "Mistress has asked me to give you some overalls, so I'm guessing you'll be staying. You're doing a great job with the garden."

The man opened the carrier bag and looked. A brand new pair of red overalls were folded neatly inside, they were the perfect size and of heavy duty cotton, obviously good quality.

"Thank you," Xu Wei managed to reply, slightly in awe of the gift, "These are very good."

Arriving home a little after six that evening, Xu Wei took out his new overalls to show to Li Yang.

"These will save my trousers," he stated proudly, "See what my new employer has provided for me."

His wife was impressed and touched the garment lightly, "What does that woman do?"

"For work?" Xu Wei replied, "I really have no idea. She always wears business suits though."

"Didn't you ask the maid?" Li Yang scolded, always the first to want information on any new employer.

"I seldom talk to anyone," Xu Wei confessed, "I just stay in the garden, eat my lunch outside and enjoy the fresh air. Today the boss lady came out to see what I was doing but mostly I work alone."

"But she has a big car?" Yang pondered, "So she must have an important job. Like a banker perhaps?"

Xu Wei shrugged and poured himself a cup of water, "I don't know dear, I don't know anything."

Another month passed without change. Li Yang continued to work weekdays for the Peel family, while Xu Wei went to the factory Monday to Friday and set off for Frau Henckel's beautiful home every Saturday.

On this particular day, however, something unusual happened.

"Xu Wei," called the maid, now beginning to relax the degree of formality that she'd shown the gardener in the first few weeks, "There is a note for you from Frau Henckel."

He took out his glasses, held up the note and read slowly, curiosity mingled with the fear that his services may no longer be required. The note was written in perfectly formed Chinese characters, and signed by his employer.

"Due to a private party here next Saturday, you will not be required to work on that day," he read, "However, due to the short notice and inconvenience, I would be happy to pay you to work on Sunday instead. Many thanks, Frau Henckel."

Xu Wei scratched his head and pushed the note deep into his overall pocket, he really didn't mind which day he came to attend to the gardens here, such was his contentment & satisfaction with the job.

"Xie xie," he thanked the maid, turning back to his task of pushing a heavy lawn-mower across the grass.

"Mei wen ti," she mumbled, going back indoors, "No problem." The following day was Sunday.

The expectation of a peaceful day at home was shattered at seven o'clock in the morning with Xu Wei waking to shouts coming from the kitchen.

"Hey, hey," he yelled, padding sleepily into the hallway, "What's going on?"

"See now," Li Yang was telling her son, "Now you've woken up your father."

Xu Bo turned red-faced to meet his father's enquiring eyes, "Dui bu qi (I'm sorry)."

"What's going on?" Xu Wei demanded, ignoring his son's apology, "Have you been out again?"

"Father," Xu Bo pleaded, lowering his voice, "It's normal for young men of my age to go out late at the weekend. I just want to have some fun."

"Fun?" scolded Li Yang, her tone shrill and piercing, "Are you not able to have fun in daylight hours?"

"Please," Xu Wei shouted, slamming his fist down on to the table, "Stop this. Xu Bo you will keep decent hours while you live under our roof. And who are you out with all night? I demand to know."

The young man glowered, his cheeks burning as he avoided his parent's stares.

"Friends, that's all," he finally told them, "Now I'm tired, so I'm going to bed."

"Well?" sighed Li Yang, sitting down at her husband's side, "What can we do?"

Xu Wei shrugged. He'd never experienced the freedom that modern young people craved these days as he'd been married to Li Yang at twenty-three and spent the previous six years toiling to save for the wedding hong bao, expected by his new bride's family.

"What do you suggest?" he asked, hopeful that his clever wife would hit upon a plan.

"Next Sunday," Li Yang smirked, her lips twitching slightly, "We go to People's Park to find Xu Bo a wife."

The suggestion was hardly a new one, Xu Wei had fully expected to be embroiled in a matrimonial coup of some sorts, but if finding a decent girl for their son to settle down with was the only way to curb his disgraceful behaviour, then so be it, a match-making trip would ensue.

The working week that followed was busy and tiring for both Li Yang and Xu Wei but nevertheless, determined to have a successful quest to People's Park where parents lined the avenues with details of their youngster's prospects, each evening was spent writing down information and searching for a suitable photograph of their son in attempt to attract a bride. With everything from Xu Bo's height, salary and favourite food listed on a sheet of A4 paper, by Friday night the couple were ready to carry out their plan, still concealing the plot from their oblivious son.

On Saturday morning, Xu Wei climbed into his red overalls and set off to Frau Henckel's mansion, his head full of tasks that needed completing such as tying back the bamboo and pruning the rose bushes. However, on arrival, he could see that the driveway held three unfamiliar cars and each had what he assumed to be a diplomatic flag attached to the bonnet. It seemed that his employer had visitors.

Dismounting from his scooter, Xu Wei stood for several seconds looking at the limousines. It was then, sliding his hands into his overall pockets as he gawped, that the gardener felt a slip of paper.

"Oi yor!" Xu Wei exclaimed, realising what it was, "Tai tai asked me not to come today! I'm supposed to work tomorrow instead!"

He took out the note that Frau Henckel had written the weekend before and stared at it for a few seconds.

"Well, I'm here now," he muttered, trudging up the path, "I'm sure she won't mind."

As he entered the rear garden, Xu Wei could clearly see Frau Henckel, the solidly built German, sitting outside around a patio table with her guests.

Some of the Chinese men looked familiar to the worker but not in a personal manner, he was certain that he'd seen at least two of them on television quite recently. They were all smoking cigarettes and seemed deep in conversation. The gardener stepped carefully, trying to make himself inconspicuous but was also interested in the little group. The visitors had yet to notice Xu Wei and as he deftly popped his tool bag down onto the grass, one of the men pulled out a thick envelope and slid it across the table to the German.

"Thank you Frau Henckel," he cooed, pronouncing the 'r' like an 'l' which was common in the Chinese pronunciation, and blowing a curl of smoke into the air just above the woman's head, "You have provided some very useful information, may our working relationship be a long and successful one."

Frau Henckel slid the package under the table and glanced at the stack of banknotes inside.

"Xie xie Sun Yi," she nodded, hastily pocketing the money, "Thank you. Now let us eat."

Xu Wei watched his employer rise from the table and call for the maid to bring refreshments, the wad of money bulging in her suit pocket as she moved.

"Xu Wei!" Frau Henckel gasped, noticing the gardener for the first time, "I said not today."

"Dui bu qi," the man managed, stepping across the lawn "Sorry tai tai, I forgot."

The woman sniffed and looked at her watch.

"Never mind," she said coldly, "We can continue our meeting inside." "Don't mind me," Xu Wei told her cheerfully, "I don't mind."

But Frau Henckel was already gesturing for her guests to move into the house, looking back only once to give her groundsman an icy glare and leaving him to continue his day's work.

"Something strange happened today," Xu Wei told his wife later that evening, "My new boss invited a lot of important Chinese men to have breakfast."

"That sounds very odd," Li Yang commented, only half listening as she put the final touches to Xu Bo's profile ready for the following day, "Who were they?"

"I'm not sure," her husband confessed, "But they all arrived in government limousines."

Yang stopped what she was doing and tapped the pen on the table, "Really? That's interesting."

"Very," Xu Wei agreed, "I think one might have been our city Mayor."

"Don't be so silly husband," Li Yang scoffed, "Why would our Mayor be having breakfast with a German woman in the suburbs? You're going senile."

Xu Wei got up and walked to the window, still deep in thought, "Maybe, wife, maybe."

"Come," coaxed Yang, beckoning him to look at the details she now held, "Read this, have I forgotten anything? I've added a few thousand Renminbi to Xu Bo's salary to make him look more prosperous, and I think we should take this photo along from two years ago, he looks slim."

People's Park was a hive of activity, with both foreigners and locals enjoying the perfectly maintained gardens, selection of cafes and restaurants and, of course, the area where hopeful parents sat touting their children's profiles as though their own personal futures depended upon the outcome. The lao wai, or foreigners, who milled about, curious and bewildered by the goings on, also stopped to look at the photographs pinned to the bushes but none could make out the carefully penned Chinese characters, save for the age and salary of the youngsters being matched up. Just to complicate matters further, very few of the young people were actually present, preferring instead to pursue other activities or just stay at home where the embarrassment of their single status could be silently ignored.

Xu Bo's parents had taken the underground metro train to the city centre. Li Yang refusing to ride pillion on Xu Wei's scooter in her best dress and freshly washed hair. The couple seldom had occasion to venture on to the busy roads of Shanghai's Puxi urbanisation together, and sitting side by side on the journey here had been a very pleasurable start to their day out.

Stepping from the relatively cool but busy tunnels of the metro station, the humidity of the August day suddenly steamed up Li Yang's glasses, causing her to grasp at her husband's arm until the temporary mist had cleared. Xu Wei gazed across the park at the hundreds of citizens bustling to and fro around the central expanse, souvenir sellers weaving their way through the crowds and security guards lazily leaning against the metal barriers near the roadside as they took a rest in the mid-day sun.

"Over there," Yang pointed, placing her glasses back on her nose after having wiped them with a tissue, "We should sit by those bushes, it will be cooler and we can tie Xu Bo's photo to the branches."

Xu Wei agreed, leading his wife steadily towards the area to which she had indicated. He took out the folding stool that he'd dutifully carried with him and Li Yang sat down, leaving her husband to tie their son's profile details to the bush at her side.

"Now, we just wait," she smiled, taking the top off a flask of green tea, "Hopefully today we will meet a decent family for Xu Bo to marry into, then all of our worries will be over."

As it happened, by the end of the afternoon, they had given out contact telephone numbers to several interested parents, all believing that Xu Bo could be a possible match for their daughters.

"Lovely to meet you Li Yang," cooed one middle-aged woman as she looked down at the piece of paper being handed to her, "We will definitely call you very soon to arrange a meeting."

Li Yang smiled, "Xie xie, I look forward to it."

On Wednesday evening the call that Xu Bo's parents had been waiting for finally arrived. The parents of twenty-two year old Xiao Pan wanted to meet for dinner so that they could question the young man about his plans for the future and see if their daughter would agree to a date. Li Yang switched off her mobile phone and grinned at Xu Wei, praying with every ounce of her energy that this would be the answer to their prayers. There was, however, just one problem. They hadn't yet divulged any of this to Xu Bo.

"What?!" the young man yelled, throwing his dinner plate into the sink, "You did what?!"

"Xu Bo," Li Yang snapped, "Sit down and listen. This is for your own good. It's time for you to find a wife and have a family of your own."

"A family?" her son repeated, bewildered, "What if I don't want a family?"

Yang stepped back, confused, "Eh? Of course you want a family of your own."

"I'm enjoying my life just fine right now mother, I don't need a wife or a child."

Xu Wei coughed and tried to calm the situation before his wife flew into a temper, "Xu Bo, of course you may think you are too young right now, but in a couple of years when you're settled and happy, you'll thank us for doing this."

Xu Bo shook his head, defiant, "Wen dao yu mang," he murmured, "It's like asking a blind man for directions. A total waste of time."

Li Yang bit the skin around her thumbnail, "Six o'clock on Friday night, dinner, here."

The notification fell on deaf ears as her son reached for his jacket and left the apartment, slamming the front door as he went, leaving the couple red- faced.

"Don't worry," Xu Wei soothed, "He'll be here, Xu Bo just needs time to get used to the idea."

"Yes, he will, our son has a good heart underneath all that bravado."

"So wife?" Xu Wei asked expectantly, "What are you planning to cook?"

Li Yang tapped her nose, already starting to mellow after the argument, "Wait and see husband. It will be a feast fit for a king. Or, if not that, fit for Xiao Pan and her family."

On Saturday morning, Xu Wei clambered into his red overalls once again, his mood extremely melancholy after the night before. Li Yang was still lying in bed, wide awake, staring at the ceiling.

Xiao Pan's family had arrived as expected the evening before but, despite waiting for three hours, during which they devoured the excellent dinner provided by Yang, made small talk about the apartment and the weather and generally exhausted every topic on the price of goods in Shanghai, they did not get to meet Xu Bo. Not only did the young man not come home but he failed to answer the calls from his mother as she desperately retreated to the kitchen every half hour to enquire of his whereabouts. Finally, at nine o' clock, feeling shamed and embarrassed, Xu Wei had closed the front door behind his guests and helped Li Yang to clear away the dishes in silence.

Now, he looked forward to a day of quiet work and contemplation in Frau Henckel's garden, away from his brooding wife and the heated words that he knew would ensue once Xu Bo returned home.

"Ni hao," Xu Wei called out to the maid whom he could see washing-dishes through the large panoramic kitchen window, "It's a lovely day, although the forecast says we might have thunderstorms later."

"Ah, ni hao Xu Wei," the woman returned, immediately drying her hands on a towel and rushing to the door, "Frau Henckel asked me to give this to you. You need to sign it."

The gardener looked down at the typed letter in the maid's hand, it must have been on the counter right by the door ready for when he arrived, therefore quite important, he mused.

"What is it?" he asked.

"Can can (look)," the woman replied, "Just read it and sign it."

Xu Wei patted his pockets and realised that he didn't have his reading glasses with him, "Sorry, could you er, read it to me, I can't see it without my spectacles."

"It's a privacy agreement," the maid explained abruptly, "You have to sign to say that anyone you see visiting here, anything you hear or learn about the mistress, you will not talk to others about it."

Xu Wei let out a loud raucous laugh, "You're joking, right?"

"No, it's very serious," the women told him sternly, "Frau Henckel asks all of her full-time employees to sign this, and now you need to do it too."

"But why?" questioned the gardener, "What on earth would I. . . . .?"

Xu Wei stopped, mid-sentence, recalling the diplomats that he'd seen the previous Saturday, the hushed voices and the envelope of money passed to his employer.

"I won't say anything to anyone," he offered, shrugging his heavy shoulders.

"So sign this," the maid urged, "Or you cannot keep your job."

Xu Wei rubbed a hand through his straight black hair, causing it to stick up at the back, "But why?"

The woman leaned forward, lowering her voice and told him what she knew, "Frau Henckel is a spy."

"What?" laughed Xu Wei, "Have you been watching too many American movies?"

"Ssshhhh, please," the maid warned, gripping his arm to emphasise the importance of her words, "Please listen to me, this is no joke. Our employer gets information from foreign embassies and passes it on to the Chinese government. Didn't you recognise any of the men here last week Xu Wei?"

He nodded, "Well, I thought I did, but it just seemed so unlikely."

The woman let out a sigh and pushed a pen into the worker's hand, "Do it, for your own sake. I'm not supposed to tell you any of this but you seem like a good man Mr. Xu."

Xu Wei looked up at the sprawling mansion and then around the immaculate garden, the space in which he'd enjoyed spending the last few weeks in his own little world, away from the nagging of his wife and their own futile situation. He desperately wanted to keep this position, but if Frau Henckel's lifestyle was funded by underground activities, how could he possibly carry on?

The gardener glanced upwards, feeling a pair of eyes watching. The German stood peering at him from an upstairs window, dressed once again in a crisp white shirt and business suit. As their eyes met she smiled, the same cat-like grin that told him who was in charge.

"Give me the pen," Xu Wei said, taking the paper from the maid, "I'll sign it."

Frau Henckel moved away from the window, satisfied that the gardener would toe the line, but determined to tighten her security measures to ensure that no further contact would occur between client and employee, even if he was just a bumbling old man.

Xu Wei returned to the garden, his mind a torrent of secrets, proposals and bamboo.

Chapter Five

The Percivals

Winter had arrived. Seldom did Shanghai feel snow or hail but icy winds from the East blew a gale across the city, slowing the pace of its citizens and, seeing those who did dare to venture out, wrapped up in thick layers to keep out the cold. The blue skies were now permanently grey and heavy rain clouds had replaced the city smog, making everything appear more gloomy and dull than in earlier months.

One Monday evening in mid-November, Li Yang returned home tearful and sad, blotting her eyes with a crumpled tissue and her heart heavy with the news that the Peels were returning to England. She was going to miss Peggy so much, and Delia had been a good employer, generous to a fault and considerate towards Yang's well-being. Of course, the Peel's had ensured that they gave Li Yang an impeccable written reference, but she still couldn't help but feel that the tides were turning in her working life.

Naturally, with such an exemplary working record, the Ayi agency had found Li Yang a new full-time position but they were a young and childless couple here to make their mark on the Chinese art scene. It was the daily interaction with Peggy Peel, who could now chat with the cleaning lady very well in Shanghainese, that would leave a gaping hole in the Chinese woman's heart. Still, their departure was to be swift, wanting to return home well before Christmas celebrations, and now Li Yang was faced with building a new relationship with a different employer, whose expectations she didn't have a clue about.

"Enjoy your final week with tai tai Delia and Peggy," Xu Wei soothed, "Maybe they will return one day."

Li Yang doubted whether they would, but took slight comfort in her husband's words, knowing that he meant well and cared about her feelings.

"One more week and they will be gone," she simpered, recalling the happy days spent out in the sunshine with Peggy and her mother, "And then I will start work for Mr and Mrs. Percival."

Xu Wei nodded, relieved in part that at least his wife would still have continued employment, he was well aware that that she worried intensely about such things, especially given the continuous anxiety that their only son gave them. There was still no improvement in their relationship with Xu Bo and the young man was now spending more and more time away from home. Xu Wei pondered whether beginning a new position would give Li Yang a distraction but he very much doubted it. Things had spiralled downwards since the attempted intervention at People's Park and now there was a void in the couple's life that desperately needed to be filled.

Tom Percival was an ambitious and talented artist, or so the agency had described him to Li Yang. His wife worked in Human Resources for an Australian company and was thirty-three years old. Therefore it would be Mr. Percival to whom Yang would report every day, his wife having already cycled off to her office in the financial district of Pudong. The ayi admired a foreigner who was prepared to take on the busy streets in rush-hour traffic, especially by bicycle, as it could be a treacherous task whatever the weather.

The couple's apartment was in a high-rise block, within easy reach of amenities and with uninterrupted views overlooking the river. From their panoramic living room window, the steamers, ships and coal tugs could be seen moving up and down the Huangpu with their heavy cargo, occasionally interspersed by the smaller passenger ferries shuttling workers, tourists and shoppers from one side to the other across the murky waters. At night, the view was something quite spectacular, multi-coloured lights from the Oriental Pearl Tower shone brightly creating an electrical rainbow in the sky and party boats in the shape of nineteenth century junks trawled up and down, providing unlimited entertainment for the revellers aboard.

On her first day at work, Li Yang stood looking up from the building's vast double doors, wondering just how many floors there were to the giant skyscraper as the top was shrouded in mist, disappearing into the sky like the tip of an aeroplane wing. She had visited only once previously, together with the agency representative who had acted as translator between Yang and her new employers, but she had been far too nervous to take stock of her surroundings on that occasion, thinking only of the questions that she must remember to ask such as salary, holidays and duties.

"Ni hao," Li Yang smiled, as the apartment door opened, "Good morning."

"G'day Yang," Tom Percival replied casually, holding a cup of coffee in his free hand, "Come on in."

Yang was unsure of the meaning of the Australian's greeting but followed her new employer into the kitchen, taking off her heavy coat on the way.

"Well," Tom shrugged, "I guess my wife showed you everything last week, so I'll leave you to it. If you need anything I'll be in the spare room painting."

He gestured towards an open door where an easel stood upon a heavy groundsheet. It was blank.

"Working on a new project today," Tom told her, "So I'll be in there pretty much all day."

Li Yang nodded to show that she understood, albeit only partly, and watched the tall Australian retreat to his work. Tom Percival was just the kind of man that she'd seen on the beach in travel agency posters, lean and tanned with shoulder-length blonde hair. She could imagine him surfing the waves without a care in the world.

"So?" asked Xu Wei expectantly, "How is your new boss?"

"Well, Mrs. Percival goes out to work in an office," Yang told him as she struggled to take off her outer clothes, "And Mr. Tom stays home working on his paintings. He's an artist."

"Yes, yes," her husband pressed, "But what are his paintings like? Does he paint landscapes?"

"I don't know," Yang confessed, "I haven't seen his work. He keeps the door closed, but I should imagine that with such a wonderful view he is probably painting the waterfront."

Xu Wei grumbled at the lack of detail and opened his newspaper, "Well, is he famous?"

"How should I know?" his wife laughed, "I couldn't tell one piece of art from another these days."

The following day, Li Yang realised that she would need to pick up a few groceries after work and reached for a large striped shopping basket that Delia Peel had given her as a gift. She was very grateful for the useful present and also liked looking at the intricate pattern, combing lots of different colours, it reminded her of Peggy when she went a little bit crazy with her crayons.

"Morning Mr. Tom," she called, letting herself into the Percival's apartment, pleased that she had been trusted with a key after such a short time in their employ, "How are you?"

"G'day Yang," came the usual response, "Help yourself to coffee if you like, it's fresh."

The ayi wrinkled her nose as she entered the kitchen, "Coffee no good, bad for health."

The young Australian grinned and poured himself another full mug, inhaling the strong aroma as he did so.

"Right," he told Yang, "I'll get started. See you later and just shout if you need anything."

Li Yang doubted whether she would need anything at all but answered in the affirmative anyway.

After lunch, Tom Percival emerged from the guest room, a paintbrush still clasped between his moving lips.

"Ah mate," he was saying into a mobile phone, "I've lost me mojo, I can't seem to find inspiration."

Li Yang was polishing the living room shelves and her ears pricked up.

"If I don't get something finished soon I'll have to start looking for a proper job."

Tom was walking out into the hallway now and suddenly stopped in his tracks, staring straight ahead at the coat hooks, something obviously catching his eye.

"Listen mate, I'll call you later, something's just come up."

The ayi turned to see what her employer was looking at but couldn't see anything, although she could hear the sound of the man's phone clicking.

"You little beauty," Tom was muttering to himself, "Absolutely bloody perfect."

Yang carried on with her work, bewildered but unconcerned.

"I don't know what he does in there all day," Li Yang was telling her husband that night in bed, "But it must be a masterpiece judging by the hours Mr. Tom spends painting."

"Do you think he would let you take a photo to show me when it's finished?" Xu Wei asked, curious about the Australian who just might be a little bit famous.

"I'll ask him," she replied, "I don't think he'd mind."

"Xu Bo is home tonight," Xu Wei whispered, "I heard him come in about ten minutes ago."

"Treating this place like a hotel," Yang tutted, pulling the covers up over her arms and turning over.

"At least he's here," her husband pointed out, "So for tonight, at least, we know where he is."

Li Yang was already asleep, beginning to dream about the boats on the river, tanned surfers on a pure white sandy beach and Mrs. Percival peddling along the busy streets of Shanghai.

"Goodnight," Xu Wei whispered, leaning over to look at his bed partner, "Sleep well."

By the end of her first week working for the Percivals„ Li Yang had established a routine. She hadn't seen the mistress at all, but the tasks were straightforward and the conditions pleasant. Mr. Tom, as she called him, kept out of the way for most of the day, but on the occasion that they did exchange a few words it was always accompanied by a smile from both parties.

"I've finished Yang!" came the announcement at four o'clock on Friday, "And it's all thanks to you."

"Ma?" Yang questioned, looking up from her task, "I'm sorry I ......"

"Oh, never mind," Tom gushed, rubbing a hand through his golden locks, "It doesn't matter."

Yang looked towards the easel, now visible through the open doorway, something bright and colourful was propped up on the stand.

"Yang see?" she asked, pointing towards Tom's work, "My husband like..." her words trailed off as she struggled to find the words to express Xu Wei's admiration for art.

"Oh, yeah," Tom Percival told her, proudly leading the way to where his finished painting stood, "Be my guest Yang, I'm pretty proud of this one."

Yang padded across the threshold, careful not to knock the palette as she entered.

There, on the artist's canvas, was a brightly coloured network of intricate colours, intersecting each other like a street plan but random enough that it followed no particular design.

Li Yang turned her head on one side, trying to get some perspective on what the painting actually was.

"Very good," she finally managed, still unable to make neither head nor tail of the image, "Bright."

"Yeah," the young Australian said slowly, "It is bright isn't it?"

Yang glanced at her watch and realised that it was time to leave, "Yang go home," she said simply.

"Cool," Tom replied, still staring ahead the artwork that he'd managed to produce, "See you Monday."

Li Yang put on her warm coat and hooked her handbag over her arm, still wondering why the canvas was disturbing her and why it really didn't resemble anything at all.

"Finished," Li Yang, told Xu Wei about her employer's work, "But I forgot to take a photo."

"Oi Yor," Xu Wei scowled, "I wanted to see it. What did he paint?"

"Well, I'm not sure," Li Yang confessed, "It was just a lot of lines of brightly coloured paint!"

Xu Wei tutted and leaned back in his chair, "You never did have an appreciation for art did you?"

The following week, Mrs. Percival was at home mid-week, busily working at her computer in the living room as Li Yang went bustling in. The weather was turning colder but thankfully it was still dry, at least for now, she dreaded travelling to work on her scooter when the storms came.

"Morning Yang," Lucinda Percival said cheerfully, looking at the cleaning lady over round spectacles, "How are you? I must say the apartment is looking great."

Li Yang smiled, "Thank you tai tai."

"Has Tom been behaving himself?" the Australian woman queried, "Tom, no problem?"

"No problem," Yang repeated, shaking her head and both women laughed.

What a strange question for one woman to ask another, the ayi thought to herself.

Lucinda spent the remainder of the day working from home, occasionally making phone calls but for the most part glued to her computer screen. Tom Percival worked silently in his makeshift studio, coming out only to have a light lunch with his wife or to use the bathroom. Li Yang worked in her usual efficient manner, skirting around her employers whenever necessary and avoiding interruption unless one or the other spoke first. Just before five as she was preparing to leave, Lucinda Percival approached.

"Yang," she enquired, "Could you work next Saturday? Maybe cook some Chinese food for a small group?"

"No problem," the ayi confirmed, taken aback by the request.

"We'll be having people over to look at Tom's new painting," the Australian continued, "But don't go to too much trouble, maybe some pork dumplings? And those little duck pancake things? Whatever you feel able to do will be much appreciated."

Li Yang was delighted to be able to showcase her cooking skills for the Percival's guests, but most of all she was pleased to be getting extra money for working on a Saturday. She knew that Xu Wei would be busy in Frau Henckel's garden anyway and Xu Bo would be working at the electrical store. So, when the following weekend came around, Yang rose as soon as the wintery sun penetrated her bedroom curtains and set out for the market to buy the ingredients that she needed. By ten o'clock the ayi was en-route to Tom and Lucinda's apartment, carefully riding along with a large basket of cooking equipment balanced in the foot-well of her scooter.

"Goodness me," gushed Lucinda, looking at the bamboo steamer and cast-iron skillet that Yang was setting out in the kitchen, "All these special things you need."

Yang nodded, "Chinese cooking very special," she told her employer.

"Can I do anything to help?" the Australian enquired, hoping for a negative response as the art of Shanghai cuisine puzzled her completely.

"No thank you, tai tai," came the answer, "What time the people are coming?"

At two o'clock that afternoon, the first of the Percival's guests arrived.

Li Yang peered around the kitchen door, smoothing down her dress after having taken off her apron. There were two Chinese people, a man and a woman, and a foreign chap in his early sixties. All were making polite conversation and looking curiously towards Tom Percival's painting which now stood on an easel in the centre of the living room, covered with a silky red cloth.

"Could you help me to take the drinks please Yang?" Lucinda whispered, picking up a small tray, "A glass of sparkling wine for the guests."

"I do it," Li Yang insisted, ushering the Australian out of the kitchen and taking the tray.

Lucinda joined the little group and smiled back at her cleaning lady, feeling blessed that Li Yang was there to help out on such an important occasion.

"Thank you," she mouthed, her perfect teeth contrasting against bright red lipstick.

"No problem," Yang returned, "Yang help."

Over the next twenty minutes several other people arrived, al smartly dressed and of varying nationalities and sexes. Naturally Li Yang was very curious as to what the party would think of Tom Percival's painting, but she was kept so busy pouring beverages and handing around food that she almost missed the unveiling. At three, Lucinda rang a little bell and held up her wine glass.

"Ladies and gentlemen," she beamed with pride, "I give you Tom Percival, my darling husband."

Tom blushed and flicked his long hair back over his shoulder, "Thanks wifey."

In the kitchen, Li Yang hurriedly set down a fresh batch of prawn dumplings and went to the doorway.

"This is my first work since coming to Shanghai," Tom announced, "It's a conceptual piece entitled 'Arrival.'"

Yang watched intently as the artist pulled the silk cloth away from his work, revealing the brightly coloured painting that she was previously familiar with. She wondered what Xu Wei would say if he could see this strange network of stripes and colours, would he really think it was art?

There was a great deal of animated conversation as the guests chatted with Tom about his work, although Li Yang couldn't make out much of the dialogue as the foreigners spoke very fast and always in English, therefore she returned to the stove and busied herself preparing another tray of snacks.

"These are really delicious," a fat bald man told Yang as he chomped on a mini duck pancake, "If you ever need a job as a cook...."

Yang looked up quizzically at the guest, wondering if he was serious and if he might pay a good salary, but the man had already turned away and was listening intently as Lucinda praised her husband.

"Yang," Tom called, coming up behind the ayi as she returned to the kitchen to fetch more wine, "Help yourself to a drink if you need one."

"Yang no drink wine," she told him politely, rather shocked that he thought she did.

"No, no, of course," he laughed, throwing his head back in jest, "But there's plenty of fruit juice."

"Thank you Mr. Tom," Yang smiled, appreciating the offer and looking over at the jug of juice on the counter, "Very good."

As it happened, Li Yang was very thirsty, having been at the Percival's home for over five hours and only having stopped for one cup of green tea. The fruit juice looked delicious too, as Lucinda had added halved strawberries and slices of apple, making it very appealing indeed, so the ayi helped herself to a glass tumbler and filled it up to the top.

By four o'clock, most of the food had been eaten and Li Yang was preparing to clear up the plates. She felt slightly drowsy but put it down to having worked a six day week, on top of all the usual worry with Xu Bo. Guests were beginning to leave and Yang hoped that within another hour she could finish her duties for the day and go home.

"Can you believe it?" Tom Percival was saying to his wife as they carried empty glasses into the kitchen for Yang to wash, "Forty thousand for my first one!"

Lucinda was wide-eyed and a little bit tipsy from the wine, "I know, it's fantastic Tom!"

Yang moved to one side to allow Mr. Percival to put the glasses on the side, her ears pricking up as she tried to catch snippets of the conversation.

"Imagine if I could do one a week," he continued, oblivious to the ayi at his side, "We'll be rich."

Li Yang tried to supress a giggle, but failed, she had no idea why but all of a sudden she felt like bursting into a fit of laughter. Both Lucinda and Tom stopped mid-conversation and looked at her.

"Are you alright Yang?" Lucinda questioned, "You look very flushed." "Hee hee," the cleaning lady giggled, "I feel very funny."

The Australian woman helped Yang to a chair and looked up at her husband, "Has Yang been drinking?"

"Only the fruit juice...." Tom started, looking over at the empty glass jug, "Oh hell...."

"Shit." Lucinda cursed, realising what had happened, "Yang's been drinking fruit punch not juice, there was half a bottle of rum in there."

"Yang sick," the ayi suddenly announced, staggering across the kitchen and into the bathroom, "Ooooh."

"Bloody hell," the couple said in unison, both stifling their laughter.

"I think we'd better call Yang's husband," Tom chortled, "She'll never make it home on her scooter."

The following morning Li Yang woke up feeling as though a bomb had gone off inside her head. It didn't seem to matter which way she turned, the pain was still there and her eyelids felt heavy.

"Guo zhi ma," Xu Wei joked, poking his head around the bedroom door, "Fruit juice?"

"Mayo la," Yang muttered, laying her head back on the pillow, "No!"

It was another couple of hours before the Shanghainese woman felt well enough to rise again.

"Anyway," Li Yang was telling her husband much later as they watched television, "I heard Mr. Tom saying that he sold the painting for forty thousand Renminbi."

"You must have got the numbers wrong wife," Xu Wei chided, "It's impossible."

"I think some of those people were from a gallery," Yang sniffed, ignoring the remark, "They were dressed in very fine clothes and arrived in big cars."

Xu Wei shook his head in disbelief, "I still think you've got it all wrong."

When Yang arrived at work on Monday morning, Tom greeted her with concern.

"Are you sure you're okay?" he was asking as the ayi took off her raincoat, "I'm so, so sorry, I honestly didn't realise that Lou had made punch in that jug."

The cleaning lady shrugged, understanding just a few words of the Australian's babbling, "No problem."

Tom Percival took a leather wallet from his back pocket and took out a few red banknotes, "This is for Saturday," he told his employee, and then taking out a pretty pink card he added, "And this is where you can see my painting, in this gallery, in Nanjing Xi Lu."

Li Yang tucked the money in her purse and looked down at the laminated card. It was printed in both Chinese characters and Pinyin and showed the picture of a stately building. After a couple of minutes of pointing and squinting, it finally dawned on her that Tom was showing her where his artwork had gone.

"Thank you," she smiled, pocketing the card, "Sunday, I go with husband ok?"

The following Sunday, the Chinese couple dressed up and prepared to catch the metro train into the city centre to see Tom Percival's painting hanging in the Nanjing Road gallery. Xu Wei was particularly proud that his wife was employed by a famous artist and had spent many hours of his working week telling his colleagues at the factory about it, even slightly exaggerating upon the level of the artist's fame.

"Hurry," Li Yang, was saying, "I want to arrive when the gallery opens at ten, before it gets too busy."

"Don't worry," Xu Wei countered, pulling on his comfortable walking shoes, "We have plenty of time."

"Where are you going?" asked Xu Bo sleepily as he padded into the room in his pyjamas.

"To an art gallery," Yang gushed, quickly relaying the details, "Now be sure you're still here when we get home, and we can tell you all about it."

Xu Bo rolled his eyes and smirked, there was nothing funnier than the thought of his ageing parents wandering around a gallery and not knowing the first thing about modern art.

"Bring your shopping bag," Xu Wei told his wife, as she ushered him out through the door, "We might want to go to Carrefour on the way home."

Li Yang reached for the bag that Delia Peel had gifted her and smiled, there was nothing she'd like more than to wander around the foreign supermarket looking at the rows and rows of produce.

Nanjing Xi Lu, or Nanjing West Road as the foreigners called it, was already teeming with pedestrians by the time the couple arrived and a blustery gale was blowing through the avenue, stripping the trees of their leaves and causing shoppers to pull their coats tightly around themselves as they walked. Li Yang fought against the wind to keep her empty shopping bag from blowing around on her arm and bent her head to avoid the sharp icy wind from stinging her face.

"It's just down there," Xu Wei was pointing, "Not far to go now."

"I hope we can buy a hot drink inside," Li Yang shivered, "It's such a cold day to be out."

"But Mr. Tom will be very happy that we made the effort to come and see his painting, " her husband quipped, holding tightly onto his wife's arm, "Just a little further."

Yang quickened her step and the pair headed towards a grand, century old building at the end of the road.

"Top of the stairs and turn right," a short, bald security guard was telling them, "All the new paintings are together in that room."

Xu Wei thanked the man and led his wife up the sweeping staircase. It was certainly a very impressive place, he thought, with crystal chandeliers and gold painted cornices on the ceiling. Reaching the top, they turned right as directed and entered a long room where a row of spotlights were positioned along the wall, each shining light upon the works that hung there.

"Which one is it?" Xu Wei asked Yang impatiently, "Which painting is Mr. Tom's?"

"Shhh," whispered his wife, unbuttoning her coat as the heat from the warm room caused her to flush, "It must be along here somewhere, just follow me."

Xu Wei trudged behind Yang as she inspected each piece of art momentarily, knowing that his wife would instantly recognise Tom Percival's masterpiece as soon as she saw it. He stopped to look at a black and white painting, wondering if it had been hung upside down.

"Here," Li Yang called softly, trying not to draw attention to herself as the gallery was now beginning to fill with new arrivals, "Husband it's here."

Xu Wei trotted excitedly to her side, adjusting his glasses as he looked expectantly at the wall, stepping back and then opening his mouth in shock.

"Oi yor!" he chuckled, "Forty thousand Renminbi!"

"Shush," scowled Li Yang, "It's impolite to discuss money. Well, do you like it?"

Xu Wei put a hand to his aching side, using the other to point at his wife's shopping bag, "Oh yes, of course," he cried, "I can see where Mr. Tom got his inspiration."

Li Yang looked down, puzzled and confused, but then saw what her husband saw. Tom Percival's very artistic and contemporary painting, with its myriad of colourful stripes and cross-sections was nothing more than a mirror-image of her shopping bag!

Chapter Six

Henri Carmel

On the Friday evening that the telephone call came, Xu Bo had been home every night for two weeks. Naturally, Li Yang was in great spirits and was busy pandering to her only child's every need in an attempt to stabilise the situation. When the ayi agency rang, it was Xu Bo who answered the call.

"Mother," he yelled from the lounge, as Yang pegged up washing on the balcony airer, "Lao ban, your boss."

Li Yang dashed to pick up the telephone receiver, smoothing down her hair as she went, forgetting completely that the caller wouldn't be able to see her.

"Wei?" she said, using the customary Chinese response, "What is it?"

Xu Bo watched his mother as she listened intently to the speaker, nodding occasionally and writing down an address, replying to every question in the affirmative.

"What is it?" the young man asked inquisitively as Yang put down the phone, "More work?"

"Yes," she smiled, clapping her hands together childishly, "A Saturday job working for a French man."

Xu Bo raised his eyebrows, "Oh, what does he do?"

"I don't know," confessed Yang, "I'm sure I'll find out soon, I start tomorrow."

Xu Wei had caught the tail-end of the conversation as he wandered into the room after having a shower and frowned at Li Yang.

"That's not much notice, is it?" he huffed, "What's the urgency?"

"The man has just arrived in Shanghai," his wife explained, "He needs help to unpack etcetera."

Xu Wei sat down and turned on the television set, "Is it good money?"

"The same hourly rate as usual," Yang told him, "But I'm just glad to have some extra work."

Xu Bo dropped onto the sofa next to his father, still thinking about his mother's new employer. He was extremely interested in all these rich and affluent foreigners that were flocking to Shanghai, and wondered if he might learn some lifestyle tips from the Frenchman, he knew that they were famed all over the globe for their style and charm. Still, Xu Bo mused, he wasn't doing too badly himself at present.

When Yang arrived at Henri Carmel's ground floor apartment, she was pleasantly surprised to find that the gentleman had already cleaned the living room and was busy putting sheets on the bed.

"Bonjour Li Yang," Henri smiled leaning forward, and then quickly reminding himself that kissing on the cheeks wasn't a custom that was upheld in China as it was in Europe, "Entree."

"Morning," Yang returned, stepping inside, "I clean?"

Henri Carmel nodded and, realising that he would have to try his best to communicate with the cleaner in English, led her to the cleaning cupboard, "I went out this morning and bought everything," he explained, proud to have managed to fight the Saturday morning crowds in Carrefour.

"Very good," Li Yang told him, "I do kitchen first."

"Ok," Henri agreed, "I'll finish making the bed."

Li Yang turned to watch her new employer walk away. She guessed that by foreign standards he would be considered very handsome with his curly dark hair and tanned skin. She'd never actually met anyone from France before and wondered whether he would be easy-going like her previous English employers or a little stricter like the German ones. Still, most important was the money and if Mr. Carmel was always so pleasant, then this job would be very easy she thought.

After a couple of hours scrubbing the kitchen and putting away the new wine glasses and crockery that her employer had also purchased that morning, Li Yang turned her attention to the bathroom. By now Henri Carmel had finished in the bedroom and was busily arranging CD's on a bookshelf while listening to French love songs, unaware that his personal hygiene was causing a great deal of amusement in the en-suite.

Li Yang had never seen so many hair and body products. There were creams and lotions, gels and waxes, brushes and sprays, all of which bore labels in

French and were completely baffling to the ayi. She took each one carefully out of the box and put it away in the bathroom cabinet, firstly taking off each lid to sniff the contents. What heady aromas there were! A couple she immediately recognised as lavender and green tea but most of the jars and pots held fragranced products of which Li Yang had never encountered before and she found herself coveting the smells longingly.

A little later, suddenly hearing Henri calling, she left the task at hand and went to find out what it was that he needed from her.

"Ah, Li Yang," Monsieur Carmel beamed, "I need to go out to pick up a few things, will you be okay?"

"No problem," the cleaner assured him, "Mei wen ti."

The European put on a smart leather jacket and picked up his keys, "I won't be long."

Yang nodded and returned to the bathroom, happy to know that she could finish her work in peace.

Half an hour later, with Henri Carmel still out on his errands, the CD that was playing came to an end. Li Yang turned, immediately noticing the silence, and stared at the music system. She wasn't overly familiar with electronic gadgets but with Xu Bo working in a store that sold CD players, she was confident enough to press the arrow denoting the 'PLAY' button to let the album repeat itself and did so now to enjoy the foreign sounds that she'd been subconsciously swaying to for the past hour. It didn't matter that the ayi couldn't understand the lyrics, she found the tunes soft and merry, causing the time to pass just a little more quickly than usual.

On Henri Carmel's return, he found Li Yang humming softly to his favourite CD as she mopped the floor.

"Bonjour," he grinned, "This music, you like it?" "Hen hao," she chuckled, "Very good."

Monsieur Carmel put down the bags he was carrying and strode over to the bookshelf where the CD's had been carefully placed alphabetically.

"Yang," he told her, "When you work, you can listen to any of this music."

The cleaner stopped mopping and screwed up her face, unable to understand, "Uh?"

"Music, "Henri repeated, taking a new disc out of its case, "You listen, no problem."

He reached down and ejected the current CD, replacing it with the other, "This one is very good."

As the song began, Li Yang suddenly realised what she was being told and thanked her new employer. This was a real treat as it wasn't often that a foreign boss would encourage her to play their music and she thanked Mr. Carmel profusely. The Frenchman blushed, unable to believe that such a small gesture could have his new housekeeper in raptures of joy and he scurried off to unpack his groceries.

"Come on," Xu Wei was saying expectantly, as he pulled off his work boots in the kitchen, "Tell me all about the Frenchman."

"He's very, very nice," Li Yang confessed, "Very polite, very tidy and he lets me listen to his French music."

Xu Wei chuckled, causing a loud burp to escape, "Ha, ha, but you won't be able to understand it."

"No," admitted his wife, "But I can still enjoy the tune husband."

Just then Xu Bo returned from his shift at the electrical store and Li Yang found herself bombarded with dozens of questions about her new foreign employer. It seemed that Xu Bo had finally turned a corner and was taking a keen interest in how his mother spent her day.

"And how about you son?" she was eventually able to ask, "Did you sell many products?"

Xu Bo shrugged his shoulders and looked down at the table, "Ma ma hu hu," he muttered, using the popular Chinese idiom, "Horse horse, tiger tiger, it was so, so."

"Maybe it's time you applied for promotion," Xu Wei commented, "If you're bored you may need to challenge yourself Xu Bo. Perhaps speak to Mr. Wu your supervisor."

A fleeting look of horror crossed Xu Bo's face as his parents nodded in unison at the suggestion but he quickly recovered himself and told them that he was content enough with his lot.

"I am already tired," he whined, "No need to add extra responsibility to my workload. Besides, Mr. Wu doesn't take home much more money than I do, so it's pointless."

Xu Wei was happy to let the matter rest on hearing this piece of information. He knew full well that employees in China quite openly discussed their salaries with each other, so if Mr. Wu had divulged his earnings to Xu Bo it must be correct.

"It doesn't matter," Li Yang interjected between the two men, "We're all working so it's really not important. Although once you start thinking about taking a wife…"

Her voice trailed off as she watched her son leave the room with his hands over his ears like a child.

"Xu Bo," his father called impatiently, "Your mother's talking to you…" but it was too late, the bedroom door had closed and their son had turned on the radio.

Left pretty much to her own devices, Li Yang was enjoying her new position with Henri Carmel. If there was anything in particular that he needed doing, he would explain in English as best he could when the ayi arrived, but apart from that the Frenchman trusted Yang's intuition and experience. She had noticed a few funny foibles, such as insisting that she returned each CD to its case and then to the exact spot on the shelf after listening, but she was grateful that Mr. Carmel was such a tidy person to work for and took his few minor eccentricities with a pinch of proverbial salt. The music itself had become something of a treat to Li Yang, and she looked forward to listening to a different type of music each Saturday. Henri would tell her whether the CD was called 'Jazz' or 'Pop' or 'Classical' but she didn't take a great deal of notice, just enjoying the different styles as she carried out her chores.

After a few weeks of being employed by Monsieur Carmel, he made an announcement that gave Li Yang quite a surprise.

"Yang, my wife is coming next week."

Li Yang was taken aback. This was the first she'd heard about a Mrs. Carmel and was delighted to hear that Henri was a family man.

"Baby?" she ventured, hoping that there might be a little one to coo over.

"Non," the man shook his head, recovering himself in English "No baby but maybe soon."

Li Yang pressed his arm gently, "Very good, wife photo?"

The man threw back his head, his tousled curls jigging up and down, " Oh Li Yang, you're an angel!" he exclaimed, rushing to a box containing unpacked personal items, "Thanks for reminding me. My photos are in here, we'd better unpack them."

Yang followed her employer across the room, faintly inhaling his musky cologne as she knelt beside him.

"Let's see what we have here," he was saying, taking a silver frame out of a piece of bubble wrap.

Yang looked over at the picture and caught a glimpse of a very elegant blonde woman in a red suit. She looked like a model that Yang had seen in one of Delia Peel's fashion magazines.

"Hen piao lian," she breathed, "Very pretty."

"Hen piao lian," repeated Henri Carmel, "I'll be sure to tell her in Chinese."

That afternoon, having arranged his photographs around the apartment, Monsieur Carmel stopped his cleaning lady just as she was about to leave for home.

"Yang," he said, pausing for a second, "Would you do something for me please?"

The Shanghainese woman stood expectantly waiting for him to explain, noticing a slight flush to her employer's cheeks, "Yes, no problem."

Henri turned and stepped back into the living room, quickly retrieving a small box before returning to show Li Yang, "You see this?"

Yang nodded and waited.

"Do you think you could take it to your house?" Henri asked, seeming much shyer than he usually did when making a request, "Just keep it until my wife goes home."

"My home?" Yang queried looking at the package which Mr. Carmel had now placed inside a carrier bag, "Yang take home?"

"Yes, that's right," the man confirmed, speaking slowly to ensure that there was nothing lost in translation, "Just for one week, and then bring back."

"Ok," Li Yang shrugged, "No problem."

"But," Henri added, holding the box tightly, "No looking."

"Ok," the ayi told him, she didn't care what was in it but was certain that it contained a surprise for the man's beautiful wife, "I put under my bed."

Henri Carmel seemed satisfied with the response and loosened his grip, allowing Yang to place the parcel inside her shopping bag. He hoped that the cleaning lady's innocence would serve him well.

"See you next week," he told Yang handing her the day's salary, "And thank you."

"I see your wife next Saturday?" the ayi asked gently, curious to know whether Madame Carmel was just as pretty in the flesh as she was in print.

"That's right," Henri confirmed, "Her name is Madeleine."

Li Yang left, repeating the name over and over until she got a close enough pronunciation.

Returning home, Yang dutifully pushed Monsieur Carmel's box under her bed for safe-keeping and began preparations for dinner. The menfolk were still out and she worked steadily, humming softly, trying to remember some of the French tunes that had been on the CD player earlier in the day.

"Ni hao," called Xu Bo, kicking off his shoes in the hallway, "I'm starving, what's for dinner?"

Li Yang sighed and rubbed her hands on her apron, "I didn't know you'd be here tonight, no friends to go out with? Or perhaps a young lady? It's Saturday night."

The young Shanghainese man entered the kitchen and shook his head, "Not tonight, my er, friend is away on holiday."

"Ooh very nice," his mother cooed, "Anywhere interesting? Is it within China?"

"No, Europe," her son mumbled, now trailing off to the living room, unwilling to continue the conversation.

Yang immediately followed. A friend who could afford to go to Europe for a holiday must have a very good job, she thought excitedly, at least Xu Bo is mixing in the right circles.

"And your friend," she pursued, "Has he, or she, been away for the two whole weeks that you've been home?"

Xu Bo shrugged, "Yes, why?"

"Oh I just wondered, perhaps you could invite him, or her, to come to see us when he, or she, returns."

Li Yang stood waiting awkwardly, hoping that confirmation of the friend's sex would be forthcoming but her son was now fixated on the CCTV news.

"Xu Bo?" she pressed, "Nothing to say?"

The young man looked up quizzically for just a few seconds, annoyed that his mother was so obviously trying to extract information, "What?"

"Never mind," the woman sighed, returning to her cooking pot, "One day I will find out for myself."

Xu Bo pulled a cigarette packet from his trouser pocket and stepped out onto the balcony. Tomorrow things will go back to normal, he told himself as he stood surveying the busy streets below. Living with his parents in their tiny apartment was becoming unbearable.

As Saturday morning approached, Li Yang decided to make a special effort with her hair. She would be meeting Madeleine Carmel for the first time and wanted to give the impression that she too cared about her appearance. Not one for bothering with cosmetics, Yang was satisfied with a fresh shampoo and set and a slick of pink lipstick, after all she was still going to Mr. Carmel's home to clean.

As she locked up her scooter outside Henri's home, the ayi stopped and cursed under her breath. She had forgotten to check whether she was supposed to bring back the box that was hidden underneath her bed! Now it was far too late, as she was already five minutes late for work.

"Bonjour, bonjour," Madeleine Carmel gushed, as she grasped Yang with both hands and kissed her on both cheeks, "I'm so happy to meet you. The apartment looks great."

"Hello tai tai," Yang managed, trying to regain her composure after the unexpected greeting, "Nice to meet you."

Henri Carmel appeared behind his wife and said something in French, causing her to release Yang from her grip quite abruptly.

"Sorry, sorry," Madeleine apologised, "I forgot that it's not your custom."

Li Yang stood fixated and silent. She was in awe of the beautiful woman with her long slim legs and silky blonde hair, and her clothes were fabulous. She longed to touch the velvety fabric of the woman's dress.

"Yang, we're going to go out for shopping and lunch," Henri explained, "We'll see you later, okay?"

"No problem," the cleaning lady smiled, "See you later."

"I'll get my coat," Madeleine grinned, heading for the bedroom, "Just a moment."

"Mr. Henri," Yang whispered, "Very sorry, I forgot the box."

"The box" Monsieur Carmel repeated, then lowering his voice he leaned towards the ayi, "It's fine. Next week you can bring it back, okay?"

"Next week," Yang echoed, "But the box, for tai tai Madeleine?"

"Oh, no, no," Henri stammered, realising that the cleaner had made a natural supposition, "It's not for my wife. In fact, it's not important at all. Next week bring back okay?"

Li Yang was very confused by the muffled conversation that she'd just had with her employer but thought it typical of a foreigner to change their mind on a whim. She was certain that Mr. Carmel had said the box was for his wife, perhaps he'd decided to buy her something else instead. It was on this thought that Li Yang stopped in her tracks. She sincerely hoped that Henri hadn't found himself a Shanghainese girl on the side. What was that saying that the lao wai used, Yang thought, while the cat is away the mouse can play, or something like that? Surely not!

She watched the couple sashay out of the building, very much enraptured with each other, painting the perfect picture of newly wedded bliss. Yang pushed all thoughts of an extra-marital affair out of her mind and began the chores. No man was that good an actor she laughed.

Meanwhile, at home, Xu Bo had returned. He had the transistor radio turned up loud and was lying back on his bed thinking deeply. The phone call that he'd received just before his break that morning had turned his life upside down. He wasn't sure exactly how to take the news or what to do about it but he had a gut feeling that this was the best possible thing that could ever happen to him.

A little while later, stepping outside to light a cigarette, Xu Bo rested his head upon the exterior wall and sighed. This had been his home ever since he could remember, this tiny two-bedroomed apartment, towering over the busy Pudong streets where nobody ever seemed to sleep. In the far distance he could faintly hear a ship's horn as it made its way down the Huangpu and wondered where in the world it was going. All of his life the young man had dreamed of travelling across the globe and now maybe, just maybe, there was a real possibility that it could become reality. But what of my parents? Xu Bo asked himself. He knew that his mother would cry and his father would be furious. Eventually they would both be mortified.

Throwing the cigarette stub over the rail and watching it fall a few storeys before being carried away by the wind, Xu Bo went back inside and removed his uniform. He certainly wouldn't be needing the pale blue shirts and navy trousers denoting the electrical store colours any more, although he would keep up the façade of going to work for as long as possible or at least until fate forced his hand. He changed into a pair of jeans and a white t-shirt, pulling on Converse trainers as he prepared to leave. He'd only need an overnight bag for the time being, no need to distress his parents just yet but eventually there would come a time when he'd empty his closet for good. As Xu Bo prepared to leave he considered his financial options, it would be another week until he got his severance pay from the store and that wasn't guaranteed, he wondered if his parents had their savings in the house or in the bank.

Hurriedly entering the master bedroom, a pang of guilt fleetingly tugged at the young man's conscience. It will just be a loan, he told himself, I can put it back in ten days or so and they probably won't even know that I've taken anything. Xu Bo opened a couple of drawers and moved his parent's underwear. Nothing. He lifted the mattress, but there was nothing there either. Bending down to look under the bed, he suddenly spotted the box that Li Yang had hidden there the week before for Henri Carmel and quickly pulled the lid off. Inside lay a few DVDs labelled in French, no money or bank cards, In fact, nothing at all that could be of use to him. He threw the discs on top of the bed and, slamming the apartment door behind him, Xu Bo headed for the metro station, head down, hands in his pockets and a sinister grin playing on his lips.

Li Yang was enjoying her day. Henri and Madeleine Carmel had returned from their shopping trip laden with bags from some of Shanghai's most prestigious stores. The couple had even bought Yang a gift, some rose tea and a box of chocolate covered nuts. She was ecstatic, seldom did her employers treat her on a whim, it was usually just at Chinese New Year that she felt the generosity of their deep pockets.

"You've done such a wonderful job of looking after Henri," Madeleine reminded Yang, "It's only a few weeks ago that this apartment was dusty and bare."

"Madeleine is right you know," Monsieur Carmel agreed, slipping an arm around his wife's waist, "You have been really great Yang."

The Frenchwoman leaned back against her husband so that her hair touched his face, "Why don't you go home early today? It's almost four o'clock, you don't need to stay."

"Oh, no problem..." Yang began to say, but then seeing the couple so loved up she went to put away her duster and thanked them very much.

"See you next week," she said shyly, trying not to look at the pair as they stole a kiss, "Bye bye."

"I have to go back to France next Thursday," Madeleine suddenly called, pulling away from her husband, "But it was lovely to meet you and I hope to see you again very soon Li Yang."

"Okay tai tai," Yang managed, feeling sad that Madame Carmel wouldn't be around for a while, "Have a good trip. Nice to meet you."

Madeleine reached out a hand and Yang shook it gently, a little bewildered at the gesture.

Xu Wei was already home when Yang arrived. Frau Henckel had also been feeling generous that day and had sent him on his way a couple of hours early. Xu Wei wondered if the German might be having another one of her secret meetings but it was none of his business and the thought quickly passed.

"You're early," he commented as Li Yang came through the door, "Is everything okay?"

"Yes, very good," she replied, showing Xu Wei the tea and chocolates, "Tai tai Carmel bought gifts and I think they wanted some time alone, you know, they're a young couple."

"Do you remember when we had to try to sneak time alone before we were married?" her husband reflected, "Sitting in your parent's house waiting for them to go to bed."

Yang chuckled as she remembered those days, "Oh yes, and my father would sit and sit until he was falling asleep in his chair before letting us be on our own."

"That was just the way it was," Xu Wei shrugged, "Honour and respectability."

"Go and get changed out of those overalls," Li Yang laughed, "I'll make a start on dinner."

After stripping off in the bathroom and taking a hot shower, Xu Wei padded into the bedroom to put on fresh clothes. The first thing that he noticed was an open box on the bed. Looking more closely, he could see that it contained some discs and presumed that his wife had borrowed some of Henri Carmel's films. He picked up the box and took it into the living room.

"What time does Xu Bo finish work today?" the man called through to his wife, "Isn't it six?"

"Yes, yes, of course," Yang replied tersely, struggling to fillet a fish, "Same every Saturday."

"Strange," came the response, "His uniform is in the bathroom." "Really?" Yang screeched, "Why would he come home early?"

"No idea," her husband muttered, bending down to put a disc into the DVD player, "Maybe he took half a day off or something, although I hope he's still got some paid leave."

"Oi yor," came the voice from the kitchen, "That boy will be the death of us!"

"Come, stop fretting," Xu Wei assured her, "After our meal we'll sit down and watch a film."

Dinner was over quickly and the plates were cleared rapidly away. Li Yang was quieter than usual and it didn't go unnoticed.

"Are you still worrying about Xu Bo?" her husband fussed, "Forget about him just for tonight. I'll make us a cup of rose tea, and then we'll sit and watch one of those French films that you brought home with the chocolates for a treat."

"Films?" Yang frowned, sitting down in her favourite chair, "What French films?"

Xu Wei pointed at the television set where Henri Carmel's box was resting on top, "Those, there."

"Oh, they're not...." his wife started to explain, but she was too tired to argue with her husband for opening up the box, "Whatever, make the tea and let's relax a bit."

Xu Wei shuffled off to prepare their drinks while Yang opened the box of chocolates, it had been a long time since the two of them had sat down to watch a film together, and although they wouldn't be able to understand what the actors were saying in this one, at least they might get a glimpse of life in Paris.

"Here we go," Xu Wei smiled, setting down the rose tea a few minutes later, shall I start the film?"

Li Yang nodded, setting down the treats between them, "Yes, ready."

At first, the music came. Pop music that was repetitive and loud, and then the credits rolled onto a black background listing the actor's names, although neither of the Chinese couple watching could read them.

The first person to appear on the set was a very young Henri Carmel. Li Yang recognised him immediately and gave out a loud shriek. Her employer was totally naked and within thirty seconds had entered a bedroom and was writhing between silk sheets with four young women.

"Oi yor!" Xu Wei yelled, quickly searching for the remote control, "It's a yellow movie!"

Li Yang knew he was right, what they called yellow movies, the foreigners would call blue movies, and this was one that she'd never be able to forget.

"It's off," Xu Wei finally sighed, having worked up a sweat in his panic to save his wife further shock.

"Xu Wei," Li Yang breathed, "There is something I have to tell you. It's about Mr. Henri."

Chapter Seven

Bibi Kapoor

On the twenty-second of January, Frau Henckel announced that she was leaving Shanghai.

It was the day before the start of the Chinese New Year celebrations and her staff had been called to a meeting where she imparted the news. Xu Wei listened forlornly as his employer explained that she would be moving back to Germany at the end of the month, an unexpected move she said, but nevertheless a shock to those who stood listening to her impeccable Mandarin.

"I have prepared a red envelope for each of you," she smiled, handing out the traditional hong bao one by one, "And my secretary has managed to find new positions for you all, the least we can do considering your hard work and discretion. Thank you."

There was a brief chatter of voices as the small group received instructions about their new jobs from the German woman's assistant, and then everyone was dismissed, Xu Wei discreetly opened his envelope, flicking through the notes with a forefinger. There was a month's salary inside and the name and address of a couple who needed his gardening services after the week long holiday period. The secretary had told him that they were Indian.

"Ni hao," Li Yang called out from the living room as she heard the front door shut to, "Is that you Xu Wei?"

"Yes, yes," he huffed, pulling off his heavy jacket and woollen scarf, "It's cold outside, have you been out?"

Li Yang shook her head, "No, husband. You know I'm not working for Mr. Henri now, I can't look at him."

"What did you tell the agency?" her husband queried.

"Just personal problems, I couldn't bring myself to tell them the truth."

Xu Wei sniffed and turned to go, "But everything is okay with the Percival couple? You'll still keep working there Monday to Friday?"

"Of course," Li Yang shot back indignantly, "At least until something with a better salary comes along."

The husband disappeared into the bathroom, deep in thought. Since his wife had stopped working Saturdays, she'd still been looking tired so there was obviously something else playing on her mind.

"Wei? Can I speak to Xu Bo?" Li Yang was shouting into her mobile phone as Xu Wei came out of the shower, towelling dry his wet hair, "It's his mother."

There was a pause as the other person said something and Yang screwed up her face.

"Oi yor, never mind," she finally relented, flipping the screen off and turning to her husband, "They must have new staff at the electrical store."

"Why what's wrong?" he asked, casually combing back his hair.

"The girl on the phone said that there's nobody called Xu Bo working there," Li Yang explained, "I just want to make sure that he knows we're having dinner with the family tonight."

"I reminded him this morning," Xu Wei soothed, "He said he was working ten until six."

"Since when has he started working different hours?" his wife quickly shot back, "He's been going in at eight every morning for the past five years."

Xu Wei shrugged, unable to give a satisfactory answer, "That's what he told me."

Yang narrowed her eyes. Their son's absence from home had been even more noticeable than usual lately, staying out all night every weekend and after midnight on weekdays. The mother knew, as it was she who lay awake at night waiting for the familiar sound of his key in the lock. Usually Xu Bo's entrance would be followed by a great deal of stumbling around in the dark and then a clatter of coins falling from his pockets as he struggled to take off his tight jeans. Li Yang was afraid that if she confronted her son it would push him further away, but the pain of not knowing what he was up to was driving her to distraction. At least the young man still had his job, that was something.

"Yang?" Xu Wei was saying softly, "Hadn't we better get ready to go?"

"What? Oh yes, yes," his wife muttered, "Our family will be waiting at the restaurant soon."

"It will be very good to see our relatives again," Xu Wei continued, rubbing his wife's shoulders, "Xu Bo can meet us there if he's not back in half an hour."

Li Yang took off her slippers and put on a pair of low-heeled shoes, "Let's wait until six-thirty, it would be nice to walk to the restaurant together with our son."

Xu Wei nodded but, despite their hopes, Xu Bo didn't turn up for another six hours.

It was just after midnight when the front door clicked shut but instead of being able to sneak quietly into his room, Xu Bo found the hall light suddenly switched on and his father standing there in blue pyjamas.

"Come into the living room Xu Bo," the old man whispered, trying not to wake his wife.

"Bu father, it's so late…" the young man whined, stifling a yawn.

"Now Xu Bo, no excuses," his father insisted, "Ran mei zhi ji (a fire burning one's eyebrows) it's extremely urgent."

The youngster tiptoed past his parent's bedroom and sat down in an armchair, dishevelled and sleepy.

"We had dinner with your uncles and aunts tonight," Xu Wei hissed, "Where were you?!"

"With my friends," his son replied insolently, picking at a loose piece of cotton on his shirt, "Father I don't want to waste my time listening to old people talk about how it was in the past and how lucky we are now."

Xu Wei could feel heat rising in his cheeks but suddenly he noticed something.

"Is that lipstick on your collar?" he snapped, "Have you been with a woman?"

Xu Bo twisted his neck and peered down at his shirt, there was indeed a red lipstick stain. He wasn't sure how to handle his father's reaction and waited for the elder man to speak.

"So, tell me," Xu Wei finally sighed, "Who is she? Where does her family come from?"

The son watched his father steadily, wondering whether to lie or to finally come clean, eventually he decided on the former and bit down on his lip hard.

"Just a girl that I knew at college some years ago," he said, avoiding his father's eye, "It's not serious."

Xu Wei shuffled forward and put a hand on Xu Bo's shoulder, "If it's serious enough to be staying out this late, avoiding spending time with your family and coming home covered in lipstick my son, it's serious. Just make sure that you're careful."

"Careful father?"

Xu Wei tutted, "Yes, careful. We don't want to have the shame of an unexpected wedding if she falls pregnant with your child! Now go on, get some sleep."

The weekend after Chinese New Year, Xu Bo was up early, leaving the house before either of his parents had even got up to use the bathroom. It had been an uneventful week, mainly due to the fact that the young man's father hadn't yet divulged his discovery to Xu Bo's mother but, he feared, it was only a matter of time. He would need to be careful over the next few months, his future depended on it.

An hour later, Xu Wei was dressed in his overalls and heading off to his new gardening job. It wasn't far, in fact only half the distance to Frau Henckel's mansion and the man was grateful as he rode out into the biting wind and wintery fog.

Golden Sunshine compound was a smart gated housing complex in a quiet suburb. Having shown his letter of employment to the security official at the gate, Xu Wei was directed to white clapboard house at the far side of the community. The gardens were fairly well-tended but needed some planting work to fill up the borders. He looked up at the number on the door, fifty-two, the home of Mr. Kapoor.

"As you can see, there's not much colour out here," the tall Indian man was explaining to Xu Wei in basic Mandarin, "We'll need you to buy some plants, ok?"

"Mai wen ti," the gardener confirmed, nothing was ever a problem for him.

"My wife Bibi will be here on Saturdays," Mr. Kapoor continued, "With our two children, but mostly I'll be at work. She doesn't speak any Chinese but she can call me if there are any issues."

Xu Wei shook the man's outstretched hand and regarded the Indian's thick beard and tightly woven orange turban. He hadn't worked for an Asian before but considered that the culture of this dark strange man might be closer to his own that of the other foreigners he'd encountered through his work.

"Bibi," Mr. Kapoor was calling through the open back door, "Come and meet our new gardener, Xu Wei."

A slim woman in her early thirties stepped through the entrance, her long black hair was glossy and she had a heavy woollen shawl wrapped around her shoulders.

"My wife is finding Shanghai quite cold after Mumbai," Mr. Kapoor explained, "But she'll get used to it."

The woman smiled and offered a softly spoken 'Ni hao," before rushing back indoors away from the wind.

"So," the Indian told his new gardener, as he watched his wife disappear, "Let's talk about plants."

"How is your new boss?" Li Yang asked as soon as her husband returned home that evening, "Ok?"

"Hen hao, very good," he confirmed, sniffing the air and catching a whiff of freshly steamed fish, "This will be an easy job I think, no heavy work and the couple seem friendly enough."

"They're Indian you say?" Yang asked, "Anything you need to be careful of?"

Her husband answered in the negative, "They didn't mention anything."

"Good," the woman smiled, "Now, let's eat."

Xu Wei noticed that his wife seemed well-rested and upbeat, but didn't want to tempt fate by asking the reason for her sudden change in mood. Instead he sat down and talked about the local news over dinner.

A week passed. Xu Bo had been home a couple of evenings but spent them in his room listening to music. Intent on discovering the mystery woman, Xu Wei had been waiting for an opportunity to talk to his son alone but with long hours at the factory and Li Yang at home when he returned nothing had yet transpired. As he set out to the Kapoor's home, however, Xu Bo stopped his father in the hallway.

"Could you lend me some money?" the younger man asked, "Just for a few days."

"What do you need it for?" Xu Bo returned quickly, checking his watch, "I'm in a hurry."

"I just need to buy a couple of things," his son told Xu Bo awkwardly, "You know, this and that."

The older man mellowed, remembering how he had like to treat Li Yang when they were courting, "Yes, but it will have to be later, okay? I don't have any cash on me right now."

Xu Bo looked disappointed but managed to thank his father before watching him leave the home.

"Hey," Xu Wei called out as an afterthought, "Get dressed or you'll be late for work."

"Oh, yes," his son answered, "See you later father."

Li Yang lay snuggled up under the bedclothes, wondering what her husband and son had been talking about. She hadn't managed to hear the conversation but it was unusual for them to be chatting so early in the morning. What was even more unusual, she mused, was that none of Xu Bo's work shirts had appeared in the laundry basket for almost three weeks and that in itself was a mystery.

"Xu Wei," called Bibi Kapoor from the kitchen window, "I've been cooking, would you like some Indian food to take home to your family?"

The gardener took off his gloves and walked closer to the voice, he hadn't understood what had been said but could see Mrs. Kapoor gesturing to him and holding up a plastic container.

"There are vegetable samosas, onion bhajees and some flatbreads," she smiled, lifting the lid to show Xu Wei, "Maybe your wife would like to try?"

"Thank you tai tai," he grinned, taking the offering, "Smells very, very good."

Bibi smiled and waited for the Chinese man to walk away before closing the window, giving a shudder from the icy breeze as she did so. Shanghai was chilling her to the bone, she thought.

The Kapoor children, a girl and a boy aged seven and eight, were riding around the compound on their bicycles, unbothered by the winter air and dismal late afternoon light. They often stopped to chat to Xu Wei in the few Chinese words that had been picked up at school and he admired how easily they had adapted to the new environment. The girl had long hair, plaited tightly down her back, while the boy wore his in a top-knot, not unlike the coolies of Shanghai who had worked around the city a century ago. Xu Wei smiled as he watched the siblings race up the short driveway and push their bikes inside the open garage.

"Very cold," he said, helping the young girl to put her cycle on its stand.

"Yes," she sighed, "But mother likes to sleep in the afternoons, so we keep out of her way."

The gardener pointed to the plastic container that he'd put on the seat of his scooter, "She's not sleeping now," he grinned, "Your mummy is cooking."

The children looked at one another and skipped into the house, leaving Xu Wei to think about their previous comment. He must have misunderstood, perhaps? Cooking, sleeping, maybe the children hadn't grasped Mandarin as well as he'd thought. He thought nothing more about the comment and continued to clip back the hedge between the Kapoor's house and their neighbours. His joints ached from the damp chill but nothing that a warm dinner and hot shower wouldn't solve, the man told himself, although before going home he intended to call in at the electrical store to give his son some money. Oh to be young again, he mused, Shanghainese girls were so demanding these days, always expecting their boyfriends to buy them gifts or to pay for their fingernails to be painted. Perhaps he could slip Xu Bo a little extra, just to help him keep his new relationship going along steadily until a future had been planned.

Ping Hong Electrical Store was a large imposing building painted in blue and yellow to match its logo. It stood on a busy street in the commercial district of Pudong and sold a vast array of white goods, in fact everything from washing-machines to hair-dryers. The Ping Hong staff were mostly young and competitive, a necessary trait given that each was paid a basic salary and relied on commission from sales to top up their wages. The older generation of staff employed there were made up of executives, department managers and cleaners, leaving the youngsters to use their wits and charm to entice customers to make an expensive purchase. As with many stores of its kind, employees lacked training but were nevertheless trusted by unwitting shoppers with regard to expertise in various products. Typical of a store on the Shanghai trading scene vying to gain top place in a very competitive market.

It was here on LuJiaZui Avenue that Xu Wei now locked up his scooter and proceeded inside the Ping Hong store. It took him a couple of attempts to navigate the revolving doors before deciding to take the side entrance, a much safer and less embarrassing option. Inside the entrance were a number of signs and an escalator leading to the upper floors. Each sign was written in both Chinese characters and English. The middle-aged man knew that his son could usually be found in the television department and gave a loud sigh as he made his way upwards to the third floor as directed.

As he was ferried upwards, Xu Wei felt the sideways glances of busy shoppers regarding him with curiosity. He looked downwards and realised that his dirty gardening dungarees were causing a little too much negative attention. Still, it was too late to retreat now, he was almost at his destination and he fully intended to be discreet if Xu Bo happened to be serving a customer. The third floor was still busy with browsing shoppers, despite the late hour of almost five o'clock and Xu Wei had to ease his way through milling bodies in his search for his son.

After ten minutes scouring the department with beady eyes, the man was ready to go home. He had spotted several staff members in their distinctive blue uniforms but none that he recognised. It was a futile exercise, for all he knew Xu Bo could be in the stockroom or even on his break.

Suddenly the man felt a tap on his shoulder and turned to see a pimply youngster in spectacles.

"Mr. Xu," the slender man grinned, "Do you remember me? Jian Yu, I was at school with Xu Bo."

"Ah, ni hao," Xu Wei regarding the youngster's blue shirt and trousers, "You work here Jian Yu?"

"Yes, I've been here for a year now," came the cheerful reply, "Where is Xu Bo working now? We were all very surprised when he told us he was leaving. Mr. Xu, are you alright?"

Xu Wei had turned pale. He put his hand on the young man's arm to steady himself and lowered his voice.

"Xu Bo has left?" he repeated, wondering how he could possibly save face after such shocking news.

"Yes, that's right, about three weeks ago," Jian Yu confirmed, "Stay there Mr. Xu, I'll get you a cup of water, just a moment."

By the time the salesman returned with a cold drink, Xu Wei had already vacated the building and was riding across town towards home, oblivious to the icy rain pelting down on his back, just determined to get to the bottom of this latest revelation.

"Ni hao," Li Yang called out the customary greeting as she got up to help her husband with his wet outer clothing, "Whatever is the matter?"

"Is Xu Bo home?" the man asked abruptly, taking a look around and forgetting to thank his wife.

"Mayo la, no," Yang told him, "He doesn't finish at the store until six."

Xu Wei went into the kitchen to make some hot tea, explaining what Jian Yu had told him as he did so.

Li Yang stood motionless before saying, "It's going to be a long night husband, we will stay up."

As had become his habit of late, Xu Bo finally returned home late on Sunday night but on this occasion could instantly tell by the irate looks on his waiting parents faces that he'd finally been caught out.

"Father, mother..." he began, unsure how to proceed with explanations and excuses.

"Where have you been Xu Bo?" Yang asked, her voice shaking with frustration and tiredness.

"Out with my...." he started, but stopped mid-sentence on seeing that his father had held up a hand.

"No more lies Xu Bo," Xu Wei told his son, "I went to the electrical store. Three weeks they told me, so where have you been and what are you doing with yourself?"

Xu Bo wasn't ready to explain, it was far too soon, instead he shrugged and hung his head, "I've been hanging out with friends that's all. I hated that job and I'm not prepared to go back."

The following two weeks were fraught with tension. Both Li Yang and Xu Wei tried different tactics to try to get their son to see sense but both approaches were met with silence and distance, at least that was so on the days that he actually did come home. The situation caused a closeness that was sometimes amiss between Xu Wei and his wife and he eventually sat her down and told her about the lipstick on Xu Bo's shirt. After that, as far as the couple were concerned, they came to the conclusion that their son was dating a rather loose woman who probably had her own apartment, which in itself would explain the overnight stays and a sign that perhaps she also had money.

As the dark mornings and even darker afternoons of February arrived, Xu Wei continued to work on the Kapoor's garden. Sometimes Mr. Kapoor would leave instructions on what he wanted doing, but mostly the gardener was trusted to make logical and practical decisions. It was on such a day that something very unusual occurred.

On this particular Saturday morning, as he raked the leaves from the lawn, Xu Wei came across a rather large hole. It was bigger than a mouse would make but too small to have been dug by a dog, which led him to the astute conclusion that the Kapoor's had a rat. Realising that the issue could quickly escalate should the creature make a nest in the hole, the Chinese man rolled up his proverbial sleeves and set himself the task of tackling the problem head on. Firstly, he decided, would need to find the other end of the rat's tunnel, and from then on block it and smoke the creature out.

The Kapoor's house was built in the style of many American homes, which is slightly raised from the ground with just enough crawl space underneath to avoid flooding and sometimes can serve as a storage area. Xu Wei bent down and peered underneath. He reckoned that he could just about wriggle under the house without causing himself too much discomfort, although he was slightly freaked out at the thought of coming face to face with a great hairy rodent. As he lay down on his side, feeling the damp ground penetrate his overalls almost immediately, Xu Wei switched on a torch and looked around. There was no sign of disturbed soil in that particular area, so he crawled out and began a fresh search on the far side of the building.

Xu Wei's first impression of the underside of the rear of the house was that the Kapoor's were using it as a dumping ground. There were black plastic bin liners heaped up all along the base, some looking quite hefty and full. Rolling onto his side, Xu Wei pushed away one of the garbage bags in order to slide himself under the house but stopped as he heard a familiar clinking sound.

Pulling open the dustbin bag, the man could clearly make out a hoard of wine bottles, some green, some clear and some brown. What a strange way to get rid of your trash, he thought innocently. He continued to shine the torch around and a few minutes later managed to spot a hole about the size of a child's head.

"Ni hao," Xu Wei called, tapping on the Kapoor's back door, "Tai tai?"

"Hello," Bibi Kapoor called back, coming to the door dressed in a blue sari and heavy mohair shawl, "What is it Xu Wei?"

Xu Wei didn't know the word for rat, but pointed at the hole in the lawn and made an attempt at squeaking like a rodent, "Problem, here."

It took a good ten seconds of imitations before Bibi realised what the Chinese man was telling her and a look of fear crossed her face as she contemplated the problem.

"No Problem," Xu Wei assured the stricken woman, immediately sensing her panic, "I fix."

Bibi's shoulders relaxed slightly but then hunched up again as she caught sight of the heavy sack now lying on the garden path. She pointed at it and looked behind her furtively.

"Ah, tai tai," Xu Wei told her, "I take away."

"Yes, yes, quickly," Bibi hissed impolitely, flapping a hand at the gardener, "Now."

Xu Wei shrugged, it didn't matter to him if he got rid of the rubbish first, although he would have expected his employer to be much more concerned about a rat infestation that a few bags of glass bottles.

"Mum," a child's voice called from the kitchen, "Can I have a cookie please?"

Bibi Kapoor gave Xu Wei a last knowing look before hurriedly shutting the screen door in his face.

"Hurry, please," she told him before turning to tend to her child.

Xu Wei was far too polite to disagree and realised that today he may need to work a few extra hours in order to clear out the stored rubbish from underneath Mr. Kapoor's house.

"Oi yor," he muttered, brushing mud from his work jacket, "Why can't these people put their bottles into the communal bin like everyone else? It's going to take me ages to clear this lot away."

It was beginning to get dark by the time Xu Wei had cleared the rubbish bags and finished his task of smoking out the rat from its hole. There was only one large, dirty brown creature as it happened but the Shanghainese man knew that vermin could multiply very quickly if not controlled, the days on his uncle's farm had taught him that much. As Xu Wei began to gather up his tools, the dim lights of a city taxi flashed at him as it pulled up next to the house. The tall figure of Mr. Kapoor quickly jumped out, looking at the gardener and then at his watch.

"You are very late," he carefully commented in Mandarin, "Is there a problem?"

Xu Wei opened the hessian sack in which he'd put the rat and frowned, "Only one."

Mr. Kapoor stepped back, covering his mouth with a hand, "Oh, terrible. Thank you Xu Wei."

The gardener pointed to the communal dustbins at the back of the clubhouse, "Bottles there."

"Sorry?" the Indian replied, "Wo ting bu dong, I don't understand."

"Jiu, wine," the other man told him, still waving his hand towards the plastic dumpsters.

Mr. Kapoor looked confused, "Sorry, Xu Wei, I don't drink, not sure what you mean."

It was getting late and the Chinese man was too tired to get into a conversation about where the wine bottles had come from and simply shrugged his shoulders and motioned to leave.

"Here," Mr. Kapoor said, taking out a note from his wallet, "For your extra time."

"Thank you," the gardener smiled, he was never one to refuse some extra cash and pocketed the one hundred renminbi note immediately, "See you next week."

As the tall Indian entered his home through the front door, Xu Wei quickly stepped around the back to collect his flask of tea that he'd left there and as he did so Bibi Kapoor opened the window.

"Xu Wei," she hissed, motioning the man to come closer, "The bottles of wine....the jiu."

The Shanghainese pricked his ears at the mention of drink and looked quizzically at Mrs. Kapoor, "Yes?"

"Please, ssshhhh," Bibi put a finger to her lips, "Don't tell my husband."

As Xu Wei rode out of the compound on his scooter, he stopped at the gate to say goodnight to the young guard who was sleepily watching a film on a portable television set, his feet resting on the table in front of him. He seemed transfixed by the scene in front of him.

"Ni hao," Xu Wei called through the tiny window, "See you next week."

The guard stretched his arms and craned his neck to peer at the older man, "Ah, ni hao. I saw you moving all those bottles earlier, Lucky old man Kapoor didn't see you."

"Eh?" Xu Wei queried, "I don't follow you."

"That Bibi," chuckled the youngster, scratching his head and making the hair stand on end, "She drinks all day when the kids are at school, lonely I reckon."

The gardener's eyes widened, "Really? But Mr. Kapoor said he doesn't drink."

"He doesn't," came the reply, "She stops at four when the children come home, we see her running out to hide the bottles under the house as regular as clockwork."

"Surely Mr. Kapoor can tell if his wife's been drinking," Xu Wei marvelled.

"Apparently not," the guard told him, "Ta men tong chuang yi meng, They sleep in the same bed but have different dreams."

Xu Wei considered the old proverb and rubbed his chin, "Bibi Kapoor must be really unhappy."

The guard seemed to have lost interest in the tittle tattle that he'd imparted and turned his head back to the film, "Whatever, these foreigners bring their families over here and don't think about how they'll spend their days. They have more money than sense."

"Maybe," the gardener murmured, pushing his scooter off the stand and preparing to leave, "But I like the Kapoor's, they're good to work for, maybe she just need to find some friends."

The young lad wasn't listening and instead just waved a hand as Xu Wei rode off, "See you."

Back at the Kapoor's house, Bibi had been watching through the window and saw the two Chinese men talking at the gatehouse. She felt a hot flush surging up her neck, convinced that they had been discussing her secret.

Chapter Eight

Xu Bo

The heat in the room was stifling and at least three of the young people sitting there had nodded off during the talk, Xu Bo was no exception but he was the only one that got caught.

"Young man," the teacher scolded, throwing a pen and hitting Xu Bo on the head, "Perhaps you would care to come to the front and recite what's on the board, that's if you can stay awake long enough."

Several of the group sniggered and many turned around to look at the red-faced student.

"I'm so sorry Mr. Green," Xu Bo stammered, "It's just so hot in here."

"Well for goodness sake let some fresh air in then."

The young man was puzzled and remained in his seat, he wasn't familiar with the term 'fresh air.'

"Open the window," the man at the front of the room huffed loudly, "Now, quickly."

Xu Bo shuffled out of his chair and swung the window wide letting in a burst of cold wind.

"Sir, it's too cold now," a woman complained, "It is February after all."

"Well put your coat on then Miss. Li, "Mr. Green bemoaned, "Can we please get on with the lesson now?"

Thirty minutes later, the class was dismissed and Xu Bo followed the rest of the group to a Starbucks coffee shop situated on the first floor. He quickly checked the price list to make sure that he had enough cash to indulge in something hot and frothy and then joined the queue.

"Hey Xu Bo," one of the other male students called, "That was so funny!"

The Shanghainese man rolled his eyes and nodded, "I was literally only asleep for one minute."

"Ha," the other returned, "The trick is not to get caught. You should sleep with your head down, as though you're studying the text book. That's what I usually do."

Xu Bo grinned and punched his friend on the arm, "I just find these classes so hard you know."

"Yes well, this tuition is our passport to a new life with prospects and money," the friend assured him.

This was the second week of Xu Bo's training for his new position on the Sea Princess cruise ship. Today's class was language, where the group were learning various useful phrases in English, French, German, Russian and Italian. If Xu Bo were totally honest, he was struggling to keep up but sheer determination to pass the training was pushing him on and he vowed to study his notes carefully in the evenings. He had to attend various other sessions too, based on social etiquette, first aid and evacuation techniques should there ever happen to be a fire on board ship. He hadn't yet confessed to the others that he'd never been to sea and the issue of possible sea-sickness was weighing heavily on his mind.

"Xu Bo," a soft voice called out to him as he collected his caramel macchiato, "There's a seat here."

Huang Li was a short, chubby Chinese woman from Dalian in Liaoning Province. She'd immediately taken a shine to Xu Bo with his puppy-dog eyes and sulky mannerisms and was now patting the seat beside her.

"Thanks," the young man smiled, looking around at his other friends who were still queuing at the coffee counter, "Can we pull up some more chairs for the other guys?"

Huang Li looked over at the Filipino students behind her, "Why do you hang out with those foreigners Xu Bo? We Chinese should stick together."

"Simple," he told her, "I'll be sharing a room with those guys on board ship and most of us will be working together. You'll be in the restaurant Huang Li, so I doubt whether we'll see much of one another."

"We'll still get days off," the woman replied, pouting her lips, "And between shifts we could meet up."

Xu Bo felt sorry for the girl but once they joined the ship he wouldn't have time to look out for her.

"Look," he said gently, "Why don't you join the other waitresses over there? Get to know them. Those are the people you'll be working with, not me."

"Are you trying to get rid of me?" Huang Li scowled, "I can take a hint."

"Not at all," Xu Bo lied, "I just think it's best if you find some people from your own group."

Huang Li pushed back her chair, scraping it loudly across the floor, "If that's what you want, fine."

Xu Bo watched her walk timidly up to the group of Chinese students and gave a sigh. It wasn't that he didn't like the Dalian native, she was very kind and sweet, but he couldn't afford to have her tagging along with him, especially as he was struggling to integrate with the Filipino guys who were much fitter and outgoing than he was. Still, it was early days, he mused.

That evening, lying on top of his bed with a folder full of notes, Xu Bo tried his best to mimic Mr. Green's different foreign accents.

"Guten tag," he whispered, forcing the German words, then, "Bonjourno, Good morning."

He flicked through the loose notes, trying to remember which exercise was tonight's homework, but was disturbed by a knock on the door.

"Xu Bo," his father called, "Ni hao, your mother has made dinner."

Quickly stuffing the file under his pillow the young man shouted 'Okay" and went to the kitchen. His parents had been very quiet lately, not questioning him about his actions or whereabouts and Xu Bo knew that it was just a matter of time before they started prying.

"These noodles are very good mother," he told Li Yang, "And the vegetables are delicious."

He could feel his parents looking across the table at each other as they ate in silence, each waiting for the other to speak first. It was Xu Wei who finally spoke up.

"How have you been spending your days?" he asked, looking frankly at his son.

"I'm taking classes," Xu Bo answered honestly, the first time he'd been open with his father for a while, "Language and first aid."

Li Yang spluttered, a spray of broth from her noodles landing on the table-cloth, "Sorry? What? Where do you find the money to attend classes? Especially now you're not working."

Xu Wei put down his chopsticks and rested a hand on his wife's arm, almost as if to silence her, "It's alright wife, I'm sure our son is going to explain."

Xu Bo wished he had held his tongue but it was too late now and he stiffened his shoulders before calmly telling his news.

"I have a new job, but it doesn't start for another month yet. My employer is providing some basic training downtown, after that I'll be earning good money."

Xu Wei clapped his son on the shoulder, "Great news. But where will you be working Xu Bo?"

"All in good time," the young man winked, "Let me get my training out of the way first."

The following day Xu Bo was awake earlier than usual but lay in bed until both of his parents had left to go their work. He knew that there was a tirade of questions just waiting to bombard him but the longer he kept his job on the cruise ship secret the better as far as he was concerned. He hated not being able to tell his parents the truth, but if they found out that their only child was just about to embark on a career that would take him to the far reaches of the earth, they would try everything in their power to stop him.

Xu Bo picked up his gym bag and pulled the latch closed as he left the family apartment. A couple of hours in the gym with his new friends would help to ease his mind and possibly offer a solution to his troubles.

"We have practice at three today," Gregory told Xu Bo as they headed for the showers after an hour of using the treadmill and rowing machine, "Want to catch the bus together?"

"Yes, great," he nodded, pulling a towel from his holdall, "Meet you outside."

As they neared the bus-stop, Gregory nudged his friend and gave a knowing wink, "Maybe there lies the solution to your problem Xu Bo."

The Shanghainese man frowned at his friend and squinted, Huang Li was already there dressed in a leisure suit and training shoes.

"Hi guys," she smiled, speaking in English for the benefit of Gregory who was a native of the Philippines.

"Hi Li," they answered in unison, searching their pockets for change as the bus pulled up, "Do you have a class this afternoon?" Gregory ventured.

The woman nodded, flushing as she batted her eyelids at Xu Bo, "Hospitality training, we're learning about foreign food and how to serve it today."

"How exciting," Xu Bo joked, faking a yawn as he stepped up to board the vehicle.

"Hey," his Filipino friend hissed, digging the Chinese man in the ribs, "Be nice to her, she might prove to be useful. Go sit at the back and I'll explain my plan."

Xu Bo was intrigued and shot Gregory a crafty smile before taking a seat at the rear, "Well, come on then," he grinned, "What's the big idea?"

That evening, Xu Bo was home before his parents and was busy setting the table for dinner when his mother walked in. She looked at him suspiciously and sniffed at the aroma wafting around the kitchen.

"I picked up dumplings, vegetable fried rice and morning glory greens from Xiang's restaurant," Xu Bo announced proudly, "You work so hard mother, I thought that maybe you would like an evening to relax without worrying about preparing food."

Li Yang stooped to look at the food which was now being reheated in her microwave oven.

"Humph," she grunted, "What have you done now Xu Bo?"

The youngster shook his head in denial, "Mother! Really! I'm just trying to make amends."

Yang studied her son's face for a few seconds but couldn't tell if he was hiding anything.

"Very well," she sighed, "Your father should be here very soon, let me pour some juice to go with our supper. And Xu Bo, I hope you washed your hands."

As they ate, the trio made small talk about the cold weather, complained of the rent increases which had recently been imposed and made complimentary comments about the food. Afterwards, Xu Bo insisted upon clearing away and ushered his parents into the living room to sit down.

"So?" Xu Wei asked his wife as their son returned to the kitchen, "What's going on? He's changed."

Li Yang tapped her nose, "Xin ping zhuang jiu jiu, like a new bottle filled with old wine."

Xu Wei agreed, his wife was probably right in thinking that this was just a superficial change.

"Xu Bo," he called loudly, "I think you have some explaining to do."

The crafty youngster had been waiting for the chance to make a surprise revelation to his parents and took a deep breath, ready to recite exactly what Gregory had told him earlier that day. If his parents believed the story, things would be easier for Xu Bo when the time came to join the cruise ship in a few weeks. He'd already convinced Huang Li to go along with the plot in return for companionship on her days off. It was really quite straightforward, the Shang-hainese told himself, and anyway when they actually got on board he would be far too busy to actually carry out his promise to the young woman. Really, the lengths that some people would go to when they felt lonely!

"And so there it is," Xu Bo finished, splaying his fingers as though he had just laid out his innermost secrets, "Huang Li and I are in love."

"And you're moving to Dalian?" his father repeated, "In three weeks' time?"

"That's right," the son lied, biting his lip nervously as both parents digested the information.

"But it's so far away," Yang interjected, "And such a cold place, in winter the rivers are frozen."

"Huang Li needs to take care of her parents," Xu Bo told her, deepening the lie, "Besides, we'll come to visit at Chinese New Year."

"Once a year!" Yang screeched, putting a hand to her brow, "Impossible Xu Bo!"

"Now, now," calm down Xu Wei soothed, "We haven't even met the girl or her parents yet."

Xu Bo went to fetch his mother a cup of water, smirking to himself as he turned his back on the middle-aged couple and hoping that the rest of his life would run as smoothly as the untruth he'd just told.

"But I don't understand Xu Bo," Huang Li was telling him, "Why don't you just tell your parents the truth instead of making up such a terrible story?"

Her friend took a long drag of his cigarette and studied her face, "I can't, alright? Don't let me down Li, I'm counting on you. Remember, you'll be lonely on that ship without me, I'm your best friend."

Huang Li looked down at her hands thoughtfully. Maybe she could make new friends, although she'd always been a bit of a loner, constantly the odd one out when it came to fashion and boys too. She despised lies but desperately wanted to help Xu Bo, he was the only person whom she'd ever really cared about besides her parents and they were now long gone.

"Alright," she finally relented, "I'll do it. Tell me what I need to know."

Gregory, who had been resting his arm on Xu Bo's shoulder throughout the conversation, now moved towards the young woman, delighted that his plan was coming together.

"I can help," he told her, "I'll pretend to be Xu Bo's parents and we can act out the meeting for practice, okay? Besides, nobody knows how to fake a smile better than me."

As Xu Bo plotted with his friends, Li Yang was sitting on the end of the bed thinking.

"What if we got a bigger apartment?" she suggested, "If we had one more bedroom, Huang Li's parents could come down to Shanghai and live with us."

Xu Wei was already under the covers and ready to switch off the light, "Money is already tight,how can we afford to feed three extra people? And when Xu Bo becomes a father it will be even more expensive."

Yang bit a nail and looked over at her sleepy husband, "Then what if we move to Dalian?"

"Our life is here," came the reply, "We are Shanghai people and we don't belong in the north. Besides we would both be as useless as a spoon in a noodle pot once the temperatures fell below zero."

He had a point, the woman conceded, "Let's sleep on it, maybe a fresh idea will appear in the morning."

Oblivious to the concern that he was causing, Xu Bo rolled in at three o'clock in the morning. He'd been offered a few hours work in the city club where his friends did a few shifts and the pay was very good despite the late finish. He'd treated himself to a taxi home that night, not wanting to hang around for the unreliable bus service that ferried late night workers to and from Puxi, and was ready for bed by the time he arrived home.

The next step of Gregory's carefully staged plan was to introduce Huang Li to Xu Bo's parents, something that would either seal or ruin his fate, depending on how well the young woman played her part. They had already disagreed that afternoon, with Huang Li suggesting that they tell the truth about their new jobs on the cruise liner and Gregory insisting that Xu Bo's parents would try to put a stop to him leaving. At least if they thought their only child was just a flight away, instead of on the other side of the globe, he explained, it might appease them slightly. Xu Bo agreed with his Filipino friend's reasoning and being outvoted two to one, the young Dalian native finally relented.

Meanwhile, as Xu Bo had worked at the club that night, Li Yang had lain awake. Her mind was filled with so many different solutions to their current situation that she hardly knew where to turn. Although, perhaps she was putting the cart before the horse, she mused, maybe this Huang Li was beneath Xu Bo. After all, she was no doubt the cause of his late nights out.

Li Yang thought that she knew her son well and, if she was right in her instincts, he wouldn't marry a woman that his parents disapproved of.

Maybe the solution to all of this was to confront the young woman face to face.

"Xu Bo," his mother called as she set out three baozi, or steamed buns, for breakfast, "Chi le, eat."

Wanting to act the dutiful son for his remaining three weeks at home, the youngster crawled out of bed and staggered sleepily to the kitchen.

"Oi yor," his mother scolded, "You look terrible, where were you until 3am?"
"You mean, you heard me...." Xu Bo started to say.

"I couldn't sleep," Yang sniffed, "What with your sudden news. Anyway, I

think it's about time we met this young girl, so bring her here for dinner tonight."

"But mother," he moaned, "I don't know if she's free, it's not enough notice."

"Rubbish," Yang snapped, determined to get her own way, "With her parents far away in Liaoning Province, Huang Li must be very lonely in the city. Seven o'clock, don't be late."

"Okay," Huang Li told her friend in between mouthfuls of dan dan noodles, as Xu Bo repeated his mother's invitation over lunch, "I'll meet you at six outside Starbucks in Huai Hai Lu."

"Do you need some help sorting out your hair and clothes?" Gregory asked, completely serious, "My sister can help if you like?"

Li rolled her eyes and slurped at the broth, "No thank you. I'm quite capable of sorting out my own outfit."

"The plainer the better," Xu Bo hinted, "My parents are very traditional."

"Okay, okay," the girl told him, finally setting down the bowl and standing up, "See you later."

Gregory and Xu Bo high-fived each other as soon as the woman was out of sight and each took out a celebratory cigarette, moving outside the café to light up.

"Are you sure she's up to this?" Xu Bo asked nervously, "She doesn't come across as a good liar."

"But she's in love with you," Gregory giggled, "Any fool can see that. So she'll do it for you."

The Shanghainese man blew smoke out of his nose and considered his Filipino friend's words, the realisation that Gregory was right about Huang Li's infatuation suddenly dawning on him.

"Mother, father," Xu Bo called out as he led Huang Li into the narrow hallway of his family home, "We're here. Come and meet Li."

"Ah, ni hao," Yang greeted them as she wiped her hands on a tea towel and rushed out of the kitchen, "So nice to finally meet you Huang Li."

Huang Li could feel her friend's mother appraising her as she spoke, gliding a subtle eye over the younger woman's outfit and hair, finally settling upon the northern face that looked back at her.

"Dalian ren ma? You're a Dalian person?" Li Yang asked, already knowing what the response would be, "How do you find living in Shanghai?"

"Yes. Oh, not bad," Li answered politely, taking off her coat, "It's much more crowded than Dalian though."

Both women turned towards the living room door as Xu Wei came shuffling out, his face smiling and friendly, "Welcome Huang Li, come and sit down, please."

After a tasty supper of pork with vegetables, Xu Bo began to visibly relax a little, his tense shoulders starting to shift and the frown on his forehead disappearing.

"Tell us about your plans for the wedding," Li Yang urged after the table was cleared, "Will you get married here in Shanghai? Xu Bo's relatives are all here. I mean, we are not a rich family but it will be expected that everyone will be invited."

Huang Li was taken by surprise and it took a kick to her ankle underneath the table from Xu Bo before she offered a response, "Yes, yes. That's fine, no problem at all."

Li Yang was disappointed in her future daughter-in-law's apparent lack of interest in the upcoming ceremony and tried a change of tactics.

"So," she smiled, looking across at the plain features in Huang Li's round face, "Where did you two meet?"

"On the training course for my new job," Xu Bo jumped in quickly, "They have an office in Dalian, so getting a transfer will be easy. Li will be working for the same company."

"So, you've known each other for less than a month," Xu Wei calculated on his fingers, "Perhaps you are rushing into a decision, or is there some other reason for wanted to get married so quickly?"

Huang Li was a quick thinker and didn't want to let the side down. She formed her mouth into a soft pout and spoke softly, clasping her fingers together in her lap.

"Mr. Xu, my parents are elderly and very sick," she feigned, keeping her voice low for effect, "I need to return to Dalian as soon as possible, to be with them. And, of course, I wouldn't dream of living with my dear Xu Bo before marriage, that would be unthinkable."

Xu Wei scratched his head, churning over the words in his mind, "But surely they wouldn't give their consent to such a union without meeting Xu Bo first?"

"That's why we're planning to go there next weekend," his son explained, his face flushed and red, "I'm going to meet them on Saturday."

"Where on earth did you get the money for the flight?" Li Yang asked, worried that the youngsters were getting themselves into debt, "It must be nearly one thousand renminbi to fly up there."

"My savings," Li offered quickly, glancing at a tongue-tied Xu Bo, "Don't worry, it'll be fine."

"Zuo jing guan tian," Xu Wei muttered as he closed the door behind the young couple an hour later, "It's like looking at the sky from the bottom of a well, we're not seeing the whole picture."

Yang had followed him into the hallway to bid goodbye to the couple and looked at her husband with concern, "What do you mean? Do you think there's more to this than we can see?"

"Maybe," he admitted, "Do you think it possible that Huang Li is with child?"
"After just a few weeks?" his wife stuttered, "Would they know so soon?"

"Doctors have all kinds of new tests these days," the old man went on, "It would certainly explain the rush. I mean, why not carry on a long-distance relationship for a while? Wait and see how they feel about each other in a few months instead of rushing things?"

Li Yang was far less cynical and rubbed her husband's back, "Stop worrying, if there's a child on the way I'll find out about it very soon. A woman has a way of telling these things."

Xu Wei accepted defeat and made his way to the bathroom. As long as his wife's instinct's clicked in, he thought, the sooner they'd get to the bottom of this whirlwind romance.

As soon as the couple were outside the building, Xu Bo took out his cigarettes and lit up. He offered one to the woman at his side but she scowled and shook her head.

"How can you do that?" Huang Li asked, her face stiff and eyes narrowed.

"I've smoked for ages," the man replied calmly.

"Not that," she sighed, "How can you lie to your parents as though it means nothing at all?"

"Look," Xu Bo grumbled, "You were great in there, but if they find out that I'm planning to leave China goodness knows what they'll do. Just play along for me, it's only three more weeks."

Li nodded but didn't look convinced, "Don't you think they'd understand if you tried to tell them the truth? Your mother seems like a very reasonable woman."

Xu Bo glared at the young woman for a second and then looked at his watch, "Look I'm meeting Gregory and the others, I have to go. Will you be alright getting back to your lodgings?"

Huang Li started to confirm that she would be but the man had already turned to leave, hunching his shoulders over against the biting wind as he headed for the metro station, leaving a trail of grey smoke hanging in the air behind him. She watched him go, wishing that Xu Bo were different.

"So, how did it go?" Gregory inquired as soon as Xu Bo entered the bar, "Did they fall for it?"

"What's that English saying?" his friend replied, "Hooked, lined and sunken?"

"Hook, line and sinker," the Filipino corrected, sliding a bottle of beer across the counter.

"That then," Xu Bo laughed, "What time do you finish?"

"Around midnight," Gregory confirmed, "Oh, the boss says you can have two full shifts over the weekend if you like, same pay as last time."

Xu Bo raised the bottle of Corona and smiled, "Great, things are really starting to pick up."

"Well, be careful," his friend warned, "You're not out of the woods yet?"

"Eh? I haven't been in the woods," the confused reply came, "There are no woods in Shanghai."

The following morning, after very little sleep for either of them, Xu Wei made his wife a cup of green tea and sat down next to her at the kitchen table.

"So, what's your plan?" he asked, recognising the determined look on Li Yang's face.

"We're going to find out all we can about Huang Li," she told him, "See what sort of girl she is."

Xu Wei didn't follow and continued to pull on his heavy work boots, "And how are you going to do that?"

"Oh, not me," Yang explained, "You. You're going to follow her."

Xu Wei stopped tying his laces and leaned back in the chair. "Me? So not only do I get to work six days a week but I have to go riding around the city spying on our son's future wife."

"It'll be worth the effort," his wife assured the disgruntled man, "If she's after our savings or is a loose woman, we'll find out and then we can put a stop to the relationship. Neither of us want Xu Bo running off to live in that cold place, so we'd better find a reason to stop him."

Xu Wei pulled on his coat without saying another word, but the burden that had just been put on him was dragging him down like a ton of bricks.

Meanwhile, across town in the Qi Pu district, Huang Li was sitting talking to her fellow roommates. It wasn't often that they were all in the apartment at the same time but there was only one class that morning and time was plentiful.

"Why don't you let us help you with your hair and make-up?" a skinny Shanghainese girl asked, "And I could lend you some clothes if you like."

Li took in the girl's trim figure and couldn't imagine her own plump frame fitting into anything that belonged to the speaker, but she did want to look more attractive, if only to entice Xu Bo.

"Maybe just my hair," she ventured after considering the offer, "And a little bit of lipstick."

Another woman got up and lifted up Huang Li's long plait that hung limply down her back, "I'm sure we can have you looking pretty in no time at all Li, now pass me those scissors."

Chapter Nine

Nina & Melvin Parkes

On Thursday night, a call finally came from the agency, telling Li Yang that they'd found her the perfect Saturday job caring for two young English children. The father was a sales representative for an airline, they explained, and despite the mother not working, they needed help at the weekends while both adults attended yoga classes and Mandarin lessons together. The hours were nine until four, perfect for the middle-aged ayi.

With Xu Bo's intended marriage, Yang was delighted to have the opportunity to add to the family funds. It was tradition for the groom's parents to provide everything but she sincerely hoped that, given the circumstances, Huang Li would be content with a modest celebratory party after the ceremony. All of these considerations were on the woman's mind as she set off the following Saturday morning to meet the new lao wai, foreigners.

Nina Parkes was a slight woman, with wispy blonde hair and pearly white teeth. She opened the door of the apartment with a huge smile and led the Chinese lady into her home in a flurry of continuous chatter, switching clumsily between English and Mandarin as she caught sight of Li Yang's confused face.

"Dui bu qi," she giggled, "Sorry Yang, I forgot you don't speak much English."

"I learn a little," Yang told her, trying to keep up with the conversation as she took off her pink anorak.

"Oh, that's good," Nina replied, "Hen hao Yang."

As Mrs. Parkes went through to the living room, two boisterous young boys came tearing out of a nearby room and began jumping on the sofa. They both had straight dark hair and slanted brown eyes.

"Now these two little monkeys are Adam and Andrew," Nina told the ayi, "And they're going to be really good for you, aren't you boys?"

"Yes!" the children yelled in unison, continuing to bounce up and down, "We will!"

Li Yang was taken aback by the boy's appearance, they were very obviously Chinese. She had no idea that their father was Asian. Yang also wondered if the boys were going to be too much of a handful for her, they seemed to have boundless energy. Still, she was here now and owed it to her agency boss to at least give them a trial. Although, looking around at the neat apartment, she could see that everywhere was very tidy so they couldn't have caused too much destruction under their mother's watchful eye.

"Ni hao, hello," she smiled at the children, "Nice to meet you."

"Ah, hello Yang," a deep voice said from behind the group, as a stocky Englishman came out of the kitchen, drying his hands on a tea towel, "You're right on time. I see you've met these terrors."

Yang nodded but was too bewildered to speak, obviously the boys were adopted then.

Nina Parkes tugged at her husband's arm, "We'd better get a move on Mel, grab your gym bag."

She then turned to the Shanghainese woman, "We won't be out too long this morning Yang, as it's your first day with the boys. We'll be back for lunch okay?"

"No problem," Yang told the English lady politely, "See you later."

With a few rapid-fire instructions to the boys, mainly pertaining to the fact that she expected them to behave themselves, Nina pulled a fleece over her head and pushed her tiny feet into a pair of trainers.

"So, here's my number in case you need to contact us," she told the ayi, "And we'll see you in a couple of hours. Meeeeelllll, will you come on!"

Melvin Parkes skittered out of a side room, heaving a rucksack onto his shoulder as he did so. He winked at the boys and high-fived them, "See you later alligators."

"In a while crocodile," Adam and Andrew chimed together as their father ran out the door, "Bye!"

"So," Li Yang asked, "What would you like to do boys?"

"Watch a film?" Andrew suggested, blowing his long fringe out of his eyes.

"Yay!" Adam chirped, "Toy Story!"

Li Yang watched the boys go to a sideboard and rummage through a vast collection of DVD's.

"Drinks?" she asked, heading for the kitchen. "Milk or orange?"

"Orange juice please," came the polite replies, as the children carefully loaded the DVD player, "And can we have an apple each please Yang?"

Yang smiled to herself, already the boys were proving that they knew how to respect her.

Back at home, Xu Bo was just beginning to stir from slumber. It had been a busy Friday night at the city club and the balls of his feet were sore from constantly being active. He looked at his watch on the beside table and stretched his muscular arms out from under the covers. He really should rest today as he had another long shift tonight but the temptation to go out shopping for new clothes was too great and he slipped his toes out into the open.

The extra cash that he'd been earning was proving to be a God-send, as not only did it help to fund the smoking and drinking that he did with his friends but there was also plenty left to buy the bits and pieces that he'd need for his spare time aboard the cruise ship. Mr. Green had told the class that they would be expected to work five days on and then have one day off, and Xu Bo fully intended to make the most of his free time. He'd been told that crew could use the gym facilities, swimming pool and games rooms at leisure, as well as being able to go onto the mainland if their day off happened to fall at a time when the ship had arrived at a port. For those days, he would need smart shorts and cotton shirts, as these were the days on which he would get to explore the world outside of Shanghai.

Making his way into the city by metro train an hour later, Xu Bo looked around at all the unhappy faces sitting around him. Some people were sleeping and would undoubtedly miss their train stop but many were just staring at the automated advertising screens on the carriage walls, expressionless as though the information wasn't really sinking in. He puffed out his chest slightly, unaware that he was doing it, proud in the knowledge that very soon he would be far away from the humdrum lives of his fellow citizens, and off to a new and exciting adventure that would take him goodness only knew where.

Beep beep. Beep.

The young man withdrew his mobile phone from a pocket and looked at the message. It was from Huang Li.

'CAN YOU MEET ME TODAY?' it read.

Xu Bo tapped the 'Delete' button and shoved the device back into his jacket. He couldn't be bothered to listen to Li's wittering today and certainly didn't want her tagging along while he tried on new clothes.

'I'll call her tomorrow, if I remember,' he said to himself, holding on tightly to the overhead bar as the underground train came to a juddering halt, sending several passengers knocking in to each other.

"Girl trouble," grinned a toothless old man, who'd been peering at the text message over Xu Bo's shoulder.

"Something like that," he shrugged, preparing to leave the train, "Nothing I can't handle."

Meanwhile, at Nina and Melvin's apartment, their new ayi was in a pickle. Adam and Andrew had decided to act out the scenes from the 'Toy Story' film that they'd all been watching, Adam taking the role of Buzz Lightyear the astronaut, while his brother morphed into the character of Woody the cowboy.

"You can be Mrs. Potato Head," Andrew instructed Yang, despite her being unable to understand what he was telling her, "I just need to get something from outside."

Li Yang craned her neck as she heard the balcony door open, hoping that the six year old wasn't getting up to mischief, but he was soon back carrying a washing-line.

"Ay?" she enquired, "What are you doing?"

"Don't worry, you'll be fine," the boy told her calmly, "Just stand still."

Before she had time to comprehend what was going on, the two youngsters had wrapped the plastic line around her several times, pulling it tighter and tighter as they circled the ayi's body. Within minutes, Li Yang was well and truly trussed up, unable to move her arms or legs. She tried to stay calm, not wanting to reprimand the boys on their first day in her care, but she could feel the heat rising in her cheeks as the realisation of her situation dawned.

"Boys," she snapped, desperately trying to find some useful words from her limited English vocabulary, "Please get this off."

Seeing their minder flushing at her predicament the boys burst into fits of laughter and bounced once again on the sofa, chuckling as they squashed the padded covers.

"Look what you've done Andrew," the seven year-old told his brother, "It's your fault."

"No it's not," laughed his sibling, flinging a cushion across the room, "You did it."

"Please, stop," the ayi pleaded desperately, wriggling her arms to get free, "Mummy will be home soon."

Both children ignored the ayi's cries, preferring instead to run around the living room, pelting each other with cushions, regardless of anything in their path.

"War!" Adam announced, diving under the coffee table and rolling out the other side, "I'm a soldier."

Just then the front door opened and two mystified parents walked into the chaos.

After a couple of hours browsing the shops and boutiques that led off Nanjing Xi Lu, Xu Bo was feeling pleased with his purchases. He'd shopped at the new Esprit store and found the shirts to be a good fit, before heading to Hot Wind to buy some canvas shoes. He already knew that his first voyage would be to the Mediterranean and light-weight outfits would be a necessity but it was hard to find many summer items at this time of year when most people were still wrapped up in their winter coats and sweaters.

As he headed back towards the metro station, the young man paused outside a Starbucks café. He never could resist a caramel macchiato and it took just thirty seconds before he was joining the queue to treat himself. As Xu Bo counted out the correct change to pay for his coffee, someone tapped him on the shoulder.

"Hey," a woman's voice chirped, "Didn't you get my text message?"

Xu Bo groaned inwardly as he recognised Huang Li's dulcet tones, "Hey there, no sorry, my battery must have died. I forgot to charge my phone this morning."

As if by some supernatural instinct, the mobile phone in question suddenly burst into life, beeping loudly inside the man's pocket as a new message was delivered. The couple stood staring at each other.

"Oh, seems okay now," Li said innocently, "I'll find us a table, large hot chocolate for me please."

Li Yang sat down on a chair in the Parkes's kitchen while the Englishwoman made her a cup of tea.

"I really am sorry," she was telling the ayi, "They're usually so much better behaved than this."

"No problem," Yang shrugged, "Mei wen ti."

Nina set down two cups on the table, "My husband will take them to the park after lunch, maybe that will tire them out. I really am sorry about them tying you up Yang."

Li Yang sipped at the green tea and appraised the woman over the rim of her cup. Mrs. Parkes was a very tiny woman compared to many of the busty, curvy foreigners that Yang had encountered over the years but she obviously liked to keep herself fit, which was a positive attribute in the Chinese's mind. As Nina pitter-pattered around the kitchen heating up vegetable soup and slicing bread, she talked in simple Mandarin, explaining to the other lady how the boys had been adopted from Beijing three years ago, telling the story very matter-of-factly without a trace of humility.

"Eat with us Yang," Nina told the ayi as she set five placemats at the table, "I made the soup myself."

"And the boys want to apologise to you," Melvin interrupted, pushing the children into the room in front of him, "They're both very sorry aren't you?"

Adam and Andrew nodded, mumbling words of regret as their father gently prodded them to speak up.

"Right," he coughed, "Now let's sit and enjoy your mother's cooking."

Xu Bo was intently responding to the text message as he sat across a small table from Huang Li.

"It's so hot in here," she was saying, "I'm sweating."

Her companion looked up and frowned, "So take off that silly woollen hat."

"I can't," the woman mumbled, beads of perspiration beginning to trickle down her forehead.

"What?" Xu Bo asked, finally flicking off his phone, "Why not?"

"It's my hair," Li confessed quietly, "My roommates have cut and coloured my hair."

"Let me see," the man demanded, curiosity getting the better of him, "Take it off."

Reluctantly Huang Li put a hand up to remove the winter beanie from her head, lowering her eyes as she did so. Underneath her hair had been cut into a rough bob shape and dyed a horrific shade of orange."

"Shit," Xu Bo cursed, stifling a laugh, "Better put your hat back on quickly."

On hearing the young man's gasp, a few customers nearby had turned around to look and one or two started pointing. It didn't take long before half a dozen more had joined the chatter.

"Come on, let's get out of here," Li hissed, pulling her hat back down firmly to cover her hair, "I need to go to a proper hairdresser to get this fixed."

"What on earth did they use?" Xu Bo pressed, gulping down the last of his hot drink, "It's awful."

"Some kind of bleach, they told me it would turn blonde like the German girls on our course."

"Huang Li," the man answered, "Are you ready to travel the world? You're certainly not street smart."

During the following week, Xu Bo was full of excuses as to why Huang Li couldn't visit his parents home. Despite several invites to dinner and a suggestion by Yang that she take the girl shopping to look at wedding dresses, each was met with a polite refusal. In truth, the Dalian native was desperately trying to find a hairdresser who could turn her locks black again, but it was proving difficult to get an appointment. She was far too embarrassed to see Xu Bo's parents with her current orange bonce.

As the following weekend drew near, Li Yang sat pondering her fate on the coming Saturday.

"What's wrong?" Xu Wei asked, noticing his wife's pensive mood, "You look worried."

It was then that the whole sorry tale about being wrapped up in washing-line wire came tumbling out. Li Yang had tried to take it with a pinch of salt, but she feared what new games the two rascals might be planning for her next child-sitting session.

"I just don't know how to keep them occupied," she finally confessed, "They're so hyper-active."

"Maybe the answer is to take them to the park to let them use up their energy," her husband suggested, "A few laps of the skating dome or the climbing apparatus and they'll soon get tired out."

"Good idea," Yang nodded, "That's exactly what I'll try this weekend."

Nina and Melvin Parkes were all ready to go out when the ayi arrived on Saturday morning. Petite Nina was dressed in tight-fitting leggings and matching sweatshirt.

"Will you be alright if we eat out after our classes today?" she asked, smiling to reveal her pearly white teeth, "There's plenty of food in the fridge for you and the boys, and we've warned them to behave."

"Any mischief and you can take away the television remote control," Melvin Parkes piped up, ruffling his youngest son's hair, "We'll be back by three."

"Okay," Yang told them, trying not to give away the nervousness that she felt about being left in charge of the boys, "Have a nice day."

Adam and Andrew turned to Li Yang as soon as the door was closed, smiling up at her like two innocent angels. She stood looking back at them for a few seconds, unsure if they were genuinely intending to behave or whether another trick was about to be played on her.

As it turned out, Xu Wei was right. A few hours of climbing, roller-skating and running around the vast area of Century Park was all that was needed to calm down the two children. Afterwards, making their way back home across a busy main road, the boys grasped their minder's hands, one either side, and walked quietly back to the apartment block. Things continued to go smoothly as Li Yang prepared some sandwiches for their lunch, occasionally poking her head out through the kitchen door, just in case.

By the time Adam and Andrew had eaten and watched a few cartoons on the sofa, they were nodding off on opposite ends of the sofa, leaving the ayi to look around for something to occupy her time. She thought about giving the home a good dusting, but it was already as shiny as a new pin.

There wasn't a speck of fluff anywhere and you could almost see your own reflection in the glimmering wooden floors that had been polished to a high sheen. It was the same case in the bathroom too. The tiles were spotless and even the porcelain toilet bowl was impeccable. Li Yang wandered back into the living room and looked around as the two boys slept on.

The bookcase was lined with novels in various colours but all were printed in English, naturally, and she was unable to make head nor tail of them. There was, however, a blue leather-bound volume right in the centre which bore no title. Yang immediately recognised it as a photograph album. Pulling the soft leather gently out from where it was nested between the reading material, the Shanghainese woman sat down on a comfortable armchair and started leafing through the pages.

There were the usual group shots, family gatherings and parties, and one which was a slightly younger Nina Parkes in her wedding gown, looking innocent and forlorn. Li Yang slipped it from the plastic sheet and rubbed her thumb over the photo before turning it over, "1995" it read. Yang turned the page, expecting to see more pictures of Nina's big day but there weren't any. Instead, she saw photos of two white babies in long frilly gowns, which she guessed to have been taken at a Christian ceremony. These weren't the distinct Chinese faces of the Parkes' boys, and therefore the woman presumed them to be relatives of the couple.

As she neared the back of the album, Yang came across a few pictures of two young children which looked to have been taken in the 1970's. She could see from the wide-collared shirts and flared jeans that it wasn't a recent photo and peered down with interest. The little girl was waif-like and blonde with big blue eyes, while the boy was chubby and had a cheeky wide grin on his face. The photo was taken on a sandy beach and the Chinese lady looked at the scenery with interest, it being her first proper glimpse of life in a foreign country besides that which she'd seen on television. England looked to be a very pretty place, she thought, the skies were blue and the sand as golden as Nina Parkes's hair.

The remaining pictures were recent ones. Images of Andrew and Adam in a place that looked like an orphanage, a couple of family holidays with the foursome cavorting on the beach, at a theme park and aboard a train, and a recent Christmas celebration where the boys were sat amongst a mountain of presents with the branches of an enormous pine tree just visible in the background.

"Mr and Mrs. Parkes love these boys like their own," Li Yang mused, closing the album and replacing it on the shelf, "I wonder if they have adopted them because they can't have children of their own."

She looked across at the dozing boys and regretted complaining to Xu Wei about them. Goodness knows what terrible life they had before coming here, she thought silently, no wonder they get excited.

"Hi Yang," Nina called, slipping off her trainers in the hallway, "Have the boys behaved?"

"No problem," Yang smiled, as she looked up from where she sat at the dining table doing a jigsaw puzzle with the children, "Very, very good."

The Englishwoman raced over to hug the boys, digging into her jacket pocket for treats as she did so.

"That's what I like to hear," she chuckled, handing over a couple of chocolate bars, "Thanks Yang."

Nina listened carefully as the boys told her about their play time at the park while Melvin disappeared into the kitchen to get himself a bottle of Tsingtao beer.

"I know it's only three," the man noted, as he entered the room, "But you might as well go home Yang."

The ayi didn't wait to be told twice and jumped up to put on her anorak, stooping down to quietly thank the boys for being so good before she departed.

"See you next week," she told the family, "Bye, bye."

Outside, Li Yang let out a sigh of relief. The first week had just been a test, she told herself, where Adam and Andrew had decided to see how far they could push their new baby-sitter, but from now on things were going to be just fine. A strong gust of wind blew across the avenue, causing the woman to pull up the hood of her jacket to protect her ears from the cold. It was quiet everywhere now, as the sky turned grey and the rain gathered, most people had scurried indoors to the warmth of their homes. All except for a group of workers, who gathered near a lorry as it reversed onto the complex. Someone was moving in, or out.

Back at home, Xu Wei was more than a little annoyed. He'd finished work at the Kapoor's house and gone straight across the city to the Qi Pu district, more specifically to the street where Huang Li had told them she lived with a group of other young women. He'd sat across the road in a dumpling shop, drinking tea near the window, waiting to see if his future daughter-in- law appeared.

"Anyway," he sniffed as he warmed his hands by the stove, "She went to the hairdresser, that's all."

"Who was she with?" Li Yang quizzed, "Was Xu Bo with her?"

"No, she was alone. Please remind me why I'm following Huang Li. Do you really think she's up to something?"

Yang shrugged, "Well, maybe, maybe not. But something just doesn't feel right about this. I mean why the rush to move back to Dalian and why must Xu Bo go so soon?"

Xu Wei was already losing interest in the conversation and was lifting the lid of a cooking pot to examine the contents, "They're young, so of course they won't tell us everything. Now, are we going to eat soon?"

An hour later, as the couple sat watching a game show, the front door slammed and two voices could be heard in the hallway.

"Xu Bo?" his mother called out, "Are you with Huang Li?"

"Yes," he replied, "But we can't stay long, as we have stuff to do."

"What stuff?" Xu Wei asked, getting up to greet their guest, "Can't you stay a while?"

Xu Bo bit his bottom lip as he thought about his shift at the club which was due to start in an hour.

"I thought you were planning to go to Dalian this weekend," Yang reminded the couple as they entered the room, "Oh, Huang Li, you've had your beautiful long hair cut off!"

Li lifted a hand and touched her head as the elder woman spoke, "I, er, needed a change."

Xu Bo looked on, feeling that he was getting out of his depth with all the lies. His mother was quite right, they had told her that they were planning a trip to Dalian, but he'd completely forgotten.

"We're going next weekend instead," he fibbed, "The flight was cancelled at the last minute."

Xu Wei tutted, "These airlines are becoming so unreliable, I hope they refunded your money."

"Yes, yes," Li jumped in, "Everything is sorted out, thank you Mr. Xu."

Despite their growing concerns over the next few days, Li Yang and her husband continued to go about their daily business as usual. Some evenings they would have the pleasure of their son's company as he came home seeking a hot meal but so too was he full of excuses as to why Huang Li wasn't available to join them. As the weekdays fled by, anxiety grew but nothing was said by either parent until Friday night, when Li Yang came home with a brand new thick padded jacket for her son, concerned about the freezing temperatures of northern Dalian city. Xu Bo took the offering reluctantly, bemoaning the style and colour but left the little apartment with it tucked into his holdall. Neither parent slept again, but this time it was more due to curiosity about Huang Li's parents and hometown that any real anxiety. Both felt sure that given two nights in the inhospitable weather of China's north-eastern city he would soon be home and rethinking his plans for moving. Xu Bo liked his home comforts too much, of that they were certain.

On Saturday morning, Li Yang was distracted by her absent son and it took her a while to figure out that there was a problem as she stood outside the Parkes's apartment block with her finger on the buzzer. She'd been waiting a full ten minutes by now but still there was no answer, causing the ayi to conclude that the intercom was broken.

"Ay," a voice called, "Ni hao."

Yang turned to see the complex caretaker hurrying towards her, still carrying a primitive broom made from tree branches. He was dressed in the familiar grey uniform from the days of Chairman Mao.

"They've gone," he told her in rapid Shanghainese, "The Parkes family moved out last Sunday."

"What? That's impossible. They didn't say anything to me."

"Some officers came from the British government on Monday but the family had already gone, don't suppose you'd know why they were being investigated would you?"

"No!" Yang told him indignantly, "They seemed like a respectable family. There must be some mistake."

The man gestured towards a couple of approaching foreigners in business suits, "Here they come now."

Over the next hour, Li Yang sat in the brightly lit, stuffy office of the compound manager. She had already taken off her outer clothing and was sipping a cup of water as a translator fired questions at her as the two men pressed their enquiries forward in English.

"They want to know if you saw anything strange going on," the young woman told Li Yang, "In the Parkes's apartment."

"Strange?" Yang repeated, frowning at the translator, "Such as?"

Her words were repeated in the officer's own language before an answer was interpreted back.

"Some kind of affection between Nina and Melvin," the woman asked, unsure if she had got the gist of the enquiry correct, "Kissing or such."

Li Yang let out a snort and threw back her head, "They were a young happy couple, of course they were affectionate to each other. How much of my time is going to be wasted today? What's going on?"

The Englishmen looked at one another and spoke in low voices for a few minutes before closing their notebooks and dismissing the translator.

"Thank you Miss, Cheung, that will be all for today," one of them said, "Mrs. Li can go now."

As Yang struggled into her pink anorak once again, the two officials left the building and sped off in a car with blacked out windows.

The interpreter looked at the older woman with sympathy and took her arm, "I'm so sorry Li Yang, I know how this must be a shock for you."

"A shock?" Yang sniffed, "Perhaps if someone actually explained what was going on…"

The Young woman was silent for a moment, considering whether to tell the full story to the other lady or not. In a split second she decided that no harm would be done by explaining the situation.

"Nina and Melvin Parkes weren't husband and wife."

"Huh," Li Yang shrugged, "I know that many foreign couples don't get married these days."

"The translator squinted and continued, "They were brother and sister, carrying on an incestuous relationship over here where their family couldn't find out. Even adopting those boys illegally."

Chapter Ten

Nicholas Green

After receiving the shocking news about the Parkes family, and also losing yet another job in the process, Li Yang started up her scooter and headed across the city to talk with the ayi agency boss. Mrs. Sun was a fair woman and Yang had no doubt that she would either receive some kind of compensation or at the very least a position to tide her over until a permanent arrangement could be secured.

It was a wet and windy ride, taking the middle-aged woman over forty minutes before she arrived at her destination. In hindsight, she wondered whether it may have been more sensible to take her moped home and catch the subway train, but with it being Saturday she wanted to catch Mrs. Sun as early as possible. Reaching Qi Pu district, close to the office location, at mid-day Li Yang sat patiently at a pedestrian crossing waiting for the lights to turn green. There were hundreds of shoppers buzzing around on the streets that day it took a few minutes before the crossing cleared.

Suddenly, out of the corner of her eye, Yang saw somebody very familiar. Although the young woman had short cropped hair, she would swear on her own life that it was Huang Li.

"It can't be," Yang muttered, stretching her neck to see as she slowed to a snail's pace, "She should be in Dalian with Xu Bo."

There was much honking of horns and ringing of bells as the woman caused the traffic behind her to slow down, and Li Yang was forced to continue her journey without getting to check whether she'd been imagining things or not. It wasn't far now to the agency and just a few minutes later she was able to dismount and lock up her scooter at the side of the pavement.

Xu Bo was lounging around in Gregory's apartment, the home that the young Filipino shared with two friends. They'd readily agreed that the Chinese man could sleep there for the duration of the weekend, as they were so often used to him staying over several times every week. Gregory hadn't told the rest of the guys about Xu Bo's predicament but they were an amiable bunch and asked very few questions. The Shanghainese man did feel guilty lying to his parents about the trip to Dalian but he didn't feel that he had any alternative. Besides, there were literally ten days left now before the ship set off on its around the world trip with him aboard and, once he was far away, Xu Bo fully intended to sit down and write a long letter to his parents, telling them of his new venture and how, very sadly, things hadn't worked out with Huang Li.

On the streets of Qi Pu, Huang Li was out shopping. Her roommates were at home watching films with their boyfriends and she hadn't wanted to play gooseberry, preferring instead to browse the market and treat herself to a marshmallow-filled hot chocolate at her favourite coffee shop. Xu Bo's warning, about staying indoors in case anyone saw her, was playing on the woman's mind but she doubted whether his parents would ever get to find out that their trip was non-existent. Besides, both Li Yang and Xu Wei would be at work on a Saturday, Li mused, and none of their friends or family had yet met their son's intended bride.

Finishing her meeting with Mrs. Sun in just half an hour, Li Yang left the office with the name and address of a family who needed her to go just two hours every afternoon starting on the following Tuesday, a position that she could easily fit in after finishing at the Percival's and a job that required both cleaning and cooking skills. She tucked the paper into her pink anorak and zipped it up tightly against the fierce winds. Yang's stomach gave a familiar growl as she hurried along the sidewalk, reminding her that it was now past lunch time for most Chinese, whose custom it was to eat at a regular time every day to ensure balance and good health. Yang had to admit that she was feeling a bit light-headed after the shock of that morning's events and the lack of fluids, missing her usual two cups of green tea, certainly hadn't helped. She looked up and down the street, hoping to see somewhere cheap to eat. From what the ayi could see, it was a choice between a local noodle shop or a Starbuck's café which stood opposite each other on the busy street.

Without a moment's hesitation, Li Yang headed for the noodle shop, with her head down against the wind. She couldn't justify spending money at the coffee shop chain, with its extortionate prices and Westernised menu and neither did she like heavy sugary drinks. A noodle shop would suit her needs perfectly, and she had already spotted one empty table close to the window. Yang sat down and took off her jacket, as the air-conditioned unit was hot and stuffy from the steaming food and numerous customers packed inside. She looked at the menu and immediately settled for pork dumplings in broth, something warming and filling for such a blistering cold day.

On the other side of the street, queueing at the Starbuck's counter, Huang Li was looking up at the drinks menu, written in chalk on a huge board behind the counter. She couldn't decide what to have, there were so many delicious new flavours to try with complimenting syrups, and she failed to notice a tall figure joining the line of customers behind her.

"Afternoon Li," a deep voice said, with a hint of a Scottish accent, "It's cold out there isn't it?"

The woman turned and smiled, the voice belonged to her language tutor, Nicholas Green.

"Are you on your own today?" the man continued, raising his bushy eyebrows, "We could get a table."

Huang Li nodded shyly at her teacher. She supposed he was used to seeing her with Xu Bo and the other students, "Yes okay, my friends are busy today."

"Why don't you go and get that table over there," Mr. Green observed, pointing to a huge leather sofa by the window that was just being vacated by a young Western couple, "And I'll get the drinks."

"Okay," Li grinned, offering a note to the Scotsman, "I'd like a hot chocolate with caramel and extra cream."

"My treat," Nicholas winked, taking out his own wallet, "Quick, get that table."

Li Yang's bowl of dumplings and broth were delicious but too hot for her to eat straight away, and she sat gazing out of the restaurant window, catching glimpses of passers-by through the steamed up panes. Her eyes wandered aimlessly over to the café across the street, where well-dressed youngsters drank from large mugs and ate enormous chocolate muffins. She found it hard to comprehend how people could waste their hard- earned money on such frivolous luxuries and turned her attention back to the cooling noodles.

Meanwhile, Nicholas Green carried the hot drinks over to where Huang Li had settled herself on the sofa. He felt sorry for the young woman, who always appeared to be on the outside of the main student group. He'd noticed in class that whenever a joke were made she was last be included in the laughter and was always tagging along behind Xu Bo and his friends, rather than mixing with the glamorous Shanghainese girls that she shared lodgings with.

"So, how are getting on with the English homework?" Mr. Green enquired, sipping his cappuccino and looking at the young woman over the rim of his mug, "Finding it easy?"

"It's not too bad," Li admitted, "Just a few grammar problems that I need to figure out."

"Ah, the grammar," Nicholas tutted knowingly, "Everyone struggles with English grammar you know, even half the population of Britain struggle to get it right at times."

Huang Li looked up at him, not knowing if her teacher were teasing. She sipped the hot chocolate and looked out across the street, suddenly coming face to face with a woman who looked like Li Yang.

"Whatever's the matter Li?" Mr. Green was asking, "You look like you've seen a ghost."

"Sorry, I have to go," the young woman replied, hurriedly pulling on her coat and scarf, "Bye Sir."

Nicholas Green sat staring at the Chinese woman's retreating figure, puzzled as to what had spooked her and wondering if he'd upset her with his comment about English grammar. The tutor wanted to help, he hated to see one of his students upset, and took off out through the door just as Huang Li disappeared around the corner. She was running fast and the Scotsman knew that his elderly legs wouldn't keep up, so he stood on the spot debating whether to go back inside and rescue his coffee or to just go home. Suddenly there was a small hand on his arm and a Chinese woman in her fifties was gazing upwards.

"Dui bu qui," the tutor said in perfect Mandarin, "I'm sorry, can I help?"

"The girl," Li Yang pointed, still staring in the direction that Xu Bo's girlfriend had gone, "Was it Huang Li?"

"Huang Li? Why yes, it was," Mr. Green confirmed, "May I ask who you are madam?"

Yang peered up at the curious foreigner, with his perfect tweed suit and red bow tie, speaking to her in her own language as if were no effort at all, "She's going to marry my son, Xu Bo."

"Really?" Nicholas chortled, briefly brushing his fingers across his thick moustache, "I had absolutely no idea! I'm their language teacher, Mr. Green. I'm very pleased to meet you."

"Lao shi, teacher," Yang repeated, unaware that her son was learning to speak a foreign tongue.

"Look perhaps I'd better go," the man offered, "Leave you to go after your future daughter-in-law."

"Okay," Yang nodded, puzzled at this new revelation, "I go home now."

The Scotsman watched Yang walk back across the street, scratching her head as if confused. She reached a red scooter and began to unlock it before riding off in the opposite direction.

"Perhaps I'd better go and tell Xu Bo," the teacher pondered, fixed to the spot outside the café and becoming buffeted by the increasing wind, "Or maybe I should just mind my own business."

Mr. Green chose the latter option and quickly descended the steps to the underground station, glad to be out of the cold frosty air but still confused about the Chinese woman's reaction. Were Xu Bo and Li really a couple? Was it that the middle-aged woman had considered it inappropriate that Huang Li were taking coffee with an older man? A foreigner at that! Chinese culture will forever mystify me, he thought.

Nicholas Green spent the rest of the day at an art gallery in the city before taking the subway train home again. His thoughts were still with the young couple and the teacher pondered the Chinese woman's revelation as he slipped the key into the lock of his front door. On the one hand it was none of his business what the youngsters got up to, besides they were old enough to get married if they wished, but on the other he felt an obligation to his employees at the cruise line offices. They had a strict singles policy when it came to employing staff for the voyages and would frown upon any secret relationship between the trainees. He was quite taken aback about the whole matter in actual fact, as he'd thought that any affection was one- sided with Huang Li doing all the running, but whatever was going on he had a responsibility to ensure that they didn't board the ship as husband and wife.

Over in Pudong, Li Yang had returned home and was in a flap. She was pacing the apartment waiting for Xu Wei to return, concerned that something untoward was going on. Neither her son nor the girl had mentioned having language lessons and the look on the foreign man's face had told her that he certainly wasn't aware of their relationship, they were also supposed to be in Dalian! She had tried calling Xu Bo's mobile phone several times but it went to voicemail on each attempt. Li Yang was too exasperated to leave a message.

Mr. Green put on his tartan felt slippers and wandered over to the window where his telescope was positioned with its lens up towards the evening sky. He'd bought it just a couple of years ago when he'd taken up the teaching position in Shanghai and it was proving to be a rather wonderful hobby. There wouldn't be many stars to gaze at tonight, he considered thoughtfully, but it was always a useful tool to look out upon the colourful neon lights of the city. There was so much to see and do over here. Since getting divorced five years before, Nicholas hadn't bothered to find a new relationship. He considered himself too old for a start and at sixty-two his protruding stomach and lined features weren't exactly a lady-magnet for potential dates. He poured himself two fingers of scotch and swung the telescope on its stand, pointing it towards the mighty Nanpu bridge in the distance. Smog was descending upon the river and the cars that traversed the structure did so like tiny beetles hurrying for shelter, nose to nose and a myriad of colours. Turning the spyglass in the opposite direction, he settled the focus on an apartment block across the street, watching pigeons dancing on the roof and noting how the gutters were full of sodden leaves. The teacher sniffed and gulped down his drink in one swift motion, debating whether to fill it up again or to fix himself something to eat. It had been a strange day, one way or another, and Mr. Green had some very important decisions to make.

Xu Bo sat cradling a bottle of beer. Ever since Huang Li had phoned to tell him about his mother seeing her at the café, he'd been in a foul mood and had even smashed his phone against the wall in Gregory's kitchen. The stupid girl, he snarled, couldn't she just have kept out of sight for two days? And what on earth was his mother doing in Puxi on a Saturday?

"Look," his friend soothed, leaning on the back of the sofa, "What's done is done now, you'll just have to come up with a good story to tell your parents. Maybe you could say that you and Li just needed some time together, would that work?"

"No," the Chinese youngster sighed, "I pretty much stay out three or four nights a week now anyway, so they probably think I'm spending my time over at Li's place. Everything is such a pickle."

Gregory rubbed his face with his hands, wondering what could be done to salvage the situation.

"You've only got ten days you know," the Filipino reminded his friend, "You can stay here as much as you want until we board the ship on March the first, but in my opinion you should go home and face the music, keep them sweet until it's time to go. Here, you can use my old phone."

"Thanks. What music?" Xu Bo frowned, taking the old Nokia that his friend was handing to him.

"Ha, just an old English saying my friend, want another beer?"

Huang Li was lying on her bed, the pillow soaked in tears and her phone on the table next to her. Never before had Xu Bo spoken such harsh words to her. She knew she'd messed up the moment she locked eyes with Li Yang but maybe the older woman hadn't recognised her with her new shorter hair, maybe Xu Bo's mother would put it down to mistaken identity. Li rubbed her eyelids and looked at the clock, it was only eight but she felt exhausted after the shouting match with her friend, maybe the best thing to do was sleep on it and meet up with Xu Bo in the morning, she thought.

Huang Li pulled a couple of fresh towels out of the cupboard and headed to the bathroom for a shower. The other girls were out, undoubtedly enjoying good food in one restaurant or another, and Li allowed the water to run down her back for much longer than her usual ten minutes. She wrapped one towel around her head and the other like a sarong around her body, leaving her shoulders bare. She stepped over to the living room window to close the curtains and something caught her eye. It was just a glimmer, like a reflection of metal almost, but a few seconds later it was gone again and Li wandered off to bed.

"You should have followed her," Yang was yelling at her husband that night, "I told you there was something wrong, you never listen to me Xu Wei."

The man at her side sat in silence, churning over the events in his mind. He understood why his wife was angry, but after six full days at work every week he really didn't have the energy to go spying on their son's new girlfriend. Although in hindsight, he admitted, it might have been the best option.

"Say something," the woman continued, "What do you think could be going on?"

"I guess we won't find out until we confront Xu Bo," the Shanghainese man muttered, picking up a newspaper, "No use worrying yourself sick over it now, sit down and rest."

Li Yang stomped off into the kitchen, cursing under her breath, the last thing she needed at the moment was a complacent husband.

Xu Bo was spending his second day lazing around in the Filipino's apartment. He had a shift at the club that evening but he knew that tomorrow morning he'd have to go home and face the music. He'd only brought enough clothes for two days and after his mother's sighting of Huang Li the day before, there could be all sorts of ructions coming his way. He stretched, flexing the toned upper arms in his body and made a dash for the bathroom while it was unoccupied. He'd stayed up late the night before, watching films with the guys and the small amount of sleep that he had managed was fitful. He knew too that he'd have to face Huang Li, they needed to get their stories straight.

An hour later, after walking the short distance to the modern low-rise apartment block where Li lived with her friends, Xu Bo knocked gingerly on the door. A slim Shanghainese girl opened it on the second knock and fluttered her eyelids at the young man.

"Hey Xu Bo," she purred in her native tongue, "How nice of you to visit."

"I'm here to see Huang Li," he replied, fixing his eyes steadily on the woman's face as she leaned on the doorframe, "Is she at home?"

The girl let out a piercing high-pitched shriek as she called to her roommate, "Li, a man to see you."

Huang Li appeared at the door and stared at Xu Bo while she waited for the other woman to step aside, "Oh, it's you. I don't think we have anything to say to each other Xu Bo."

Ten minutes later, in the relative privacy of a quiet nook in the café around the corner, Xu Bo made his apologies and pleaded with Huang Li to continue the farce of lies that they'd been weaving.

"Please Li," he whined, using his masculine charms, "You're my only hope, it's not long until we start our jobs on the cruise ship and I can't risk my parents getting suspicious."

The woman scraped whipped cream off her drink with a spoon and thought for a moment. If only she wasn't so desperately in love with Xu Bo it would be easy to walk away. Finally she sighed and looked into his dark chestnut eyes, "Okay, I suppose so."

"Ah, so it's true then is it?" a man called as he strode over to the table, "You are a couple."

"No, no," Xu Bo replied hastily as Nicholas Green took the vacant chair next to him, "Mr. Green this isn't what it looks like."

"Come on," the tutor grinned, "I've seen enough young couples in love in my time. You do know it's against company policy don't you?"

"What, I, no, Mr. Green really we're not…." Xu Bo's voice trailed off as he realised the enormity of this new complication.

Nicholas Green stirred sugar into his coffee and focussed on Huang Li. Her body language, legs towards her companion, blushing cheeks and open hands, told him that she at least was infatuated.

"How about you Li?" the Scotsman prompted, "Are you going to tell me there's nothing going on?"

Huang Li stayed silent for fear of Xu Bo's wrath should she dig an even bigger hole, but her face flushed and she bowed her head.

"Look, I'll tell you what," Mr. Green sniffed, getting up again, "You've got three days to come clean with the shipping company or I'll be telling them myself. My own job would be on the line if they found out that I knew and kept it to myself."

"Mr. Green, honestly, we're not…" Xu Bo began, wanting desperately to tell his teacher the whole story.

The Scotsman was already holding up a hand to silence the Chinese man and picked up his disposable coffee cup with the other, "I don't want to hear it Xu Bo, three days, now good day to you both."

The youngsters sat in silence as they watched the foreigner make his way to the exit.

The following morning, Xu Bo returned home just after nine o'clock knowing full well that his parents would both be out at work. He filled the compact bath tub with hot soapy water and lay there until he felt his muscles begin to relax and a heavy tiredness wash over him. He had already decided that speaking to his father first would be the lesser of two evils, being a man he might actually believe the concocted story of the youngsters wanting time alone together, but now the added complication of Mr. Green's ultimatum was playing on his mind. Xu Bo still had no idea what his mother had been doing in the city on Saturday afternoon but he was too caught up in his own situation to bother to find out. After dressing and putting a large amount of gel on his hair to spike it up, Xu

Bo left the apartment again and headed off to class. Luckily for him, there were no language lessons on Mondays but he still needed to attend the health and safety class and spend another couple of hours in the gym. A busy day and a mountain of revision were not ideal stress-busters and Xu Bo returned home at tea time unprepared for what lay ahead.

"So that's the truth of the matter," he lied to his father as they spoke in hushed tones whilst Li Yang prepared the evening meal, "We just wanted a weekend alone and Li's roommates were away."

Xu Wei listened patiently. He wasn't unsympathetic to his son's plight but still couldn't agree with the way in which the couple were conducting themselves. Any girl with morals would wait until after marriage to sleep with her partner, he told his son.

"Oi yor," he finally said, "What's done is done now. So explain to me about the language lessons."

"Well," Xu Bo gulped, "That's simple. Everyone is learning English to better their career prospects these days. I have more chance of promotion if my English is good."

"Oh, so you'll need English up in Dalian?" his father pressed, "I would never have thought that."

The young man paused for a second. He'd completely forgotten that they were supposed to be moving up to the northern city. The lies would be his downfall one of these days.

"Yes, yes," he finally explained, "There are lots of foreign companies up there father."

Li Yang had appeared in the doorway behind her husband and son. She was listening intently and was feeling quite ashamed that her only child would sneak around behind their backs in such a way. Maybe she should speak to Huang Li about chastity and self-respect Yang told herself as she returned to tend to the stove, young modern women were too wayward these days.

Nicholas Green had just returned home from a meeting with his boss. He had been called in to give a progress report on the new recruits, as in just over a week they would be assigned to their cabins, given the planned rota for their shifts and the liner would sail away with their young crew on board. Mr. Green had said nothing about his concerns over the young couple as he sincerely hoped that they would resolve the issue by themselves one way or another without him having to get involved. He was too old and wise to become embroiled in a sticky situation and if they chose to do nothing, he already had two reserve candidates lined up to take their places on the ship.

Nicholas took a long shower and wrapped himself in a fleecy dressing-gown before going over to his telescope to view the Shanghai sky. The old man ran a gnarled finger over the tubular steel frame and adjusted the lens to focus on his target.

"Mmm, there she is," he mumbled, licking his lips as pushed his left eye tight up against the viewing hole, "Same time every night, very nice."

Across the street, Huang Li was alone in the apartment. Her friends were out late night shopping and she'd taken the opportunity of having an early shower while listening to some classical music. As she entered the living room wrapped in a towel, Li realised that the curtains were still open and padded over to close them. As she did so, a metallic glint caught her eye for the second time in as many days. She peered out, pressing her face against the window-pane. There was nothing to see with the naked eye, just another apartment block across the street and most of those were lit up by electric lights, the occupants going about their evening chores. But there, right in the middle, facing her own window, was a darkened room. It was from there that Huang Li suddenly caught another glimpse of the shining object.

"Oh my goodness," she squealed, clutching the towel tightly to her body, "Someone is spying on me!"

She pulled the curtains closed in one swift motion and reached for her phone.

Nicholas Green stood fixed to the spot. He was sure that Li had seen the end of the telescope poking out through the gap in the drapes but he'd been unable to draw his eyes away from her milky white shoulders and chubby arms. He was certain that there was no-one else in the apartment with the young woman and she would have no idea who lived across the street but still, he concluded, next time he'd have to be more careful. He couldn't risk getting caught.

"Hey, hey, calm down," Xu Bo was saying into his phone, "Okay, okay I'm coming."

"Whatever is the matter?" his mother urged, "Is she okay?"

"I need to go," her son shot back, grabbing his jacket, "I'll explain later."

"It'll be quicker if I take you on my scooter," Xu Wei stated, getting his own coat off the hook, "Come on son let's get going. Whatever it is she sounded upset."

Taking the steps up to Huang Li's apartment two at a time with his father huffing and puffing behind him, Xu Bo raced upwards. He banged on the door and within a couple of seconds a fully-dressed Li opened it wide, ushering him inside.

"My father's with me," Xu Bo explained, gesturing behind him, "He insisted."

"Come quickly over here," the young woman told him, "It was there, in that middle apartment, three floors up. I think someone's been watching me for a while."

As Xu Bo squinted to try to make out if there was anything across the street, his father staggered into the room and gave Huang Li a nod.

"What is it? Xu Wei asked, looking over his son's shoulder, "What happened?"

"Stay here," Xu Bo told the older man, "I'll go and take a look. Huang Li can explain everything."

With that he set off back down the concrete staircase even faster than he'd sped up them.

It wasn't difficult to work out which apartment was the one that had been in darkness. A simple calculation of the layout of the building across the street saw Xu Bo find the correct one within just a couple of minutes. He took a gulp of air and knocked heavily on the front door.

"Come on, open up," he shouted, causing several doors to open and their curious occupants peak out.

"Yes, yes, just a moment," a drunken Scots accent called from inside, "What's all the fuss?"

As the door swung open, Xu Bo did a double take. In front of him was his English teacher, clad in tartan pyjamas and slippers. He was clutching a tumbler of dark coloured spirit.

"Mr. Green," he managed to say, doing a quick check in his mind to ensure that he'd got the right location, "Sir, I need to come in."

"Och, sure lad," Nicholas Green smiled, "Were you needing a chat about your wee romantic problem?"

Xu Bo followed the tutor down the passage and into the living room where a huge contraption on a tripod took centre place in front of the window.

"You've been watching Huang Li," the Shanghainese man stated calmly, figuring it best if he remained cool and collected, "Don't try to deny it."

"Hah," Mr. Green laughed, swigging back his whisky, "You can't prove a thing."

The two men eyed each other, each weighing up the other's reaction, neither speaking. Finally it was Xu Bo that started up the dialogue.

"Neither can you prove that I'm in a relationship with Li," he said steadily, raising an eyebrow.

"Ah, so that's how you want to play this is it?" the Scotsman sighed, turning to pour himself another drink, "Alright, let's call it a truce. But if my boss finds out…"

"There's nothing to find out, honestly," the Chinese insisted, "Huang Li and I will get on that ship as single people and that's the way it will remain."

Nicholas Green nodded and watched the younger man leave, letting out a sigh of relief and certain that he wasn't going to be reported to the authorities for his peeping tom behaviour.

Chapter Eleven

Chi & Constantin Helios

After finishing at the Percival's on Tuesday afternoon, Li Yang checked the piece of paper in her pocket and set off for her new position. A couple of hours extra work would mean that she wouldn't get home until six-thirty, but Xu Wei would just have to start cooking dinner, the woman had told herself, but the extra money would be very useful. It wasn't far to the pretty white villa, just ten minutes ride on her scooter and, although it was already beginning to fall dark, the streets were well lit and not yet busy from the rush-hour traffic.

The ayi arrived at a gated complex and gave the security guard her details before being directed to the largest house on the site. It looked in perfect order from the outside and the gardens were particularly well-maintained with neat borders and a beautiful oriental feature just visible to the rear. Li Yang put a hand up to fluff her hair, which had been flattened by the crash helmet, and rang the bell.

"Ah, ni hao Li Yang," a Chinese woman smiled, opening the door wide, "Come in, it's very cold out there."

She spoke in clipped Mandarin, hinting that it may not have been her native tongue but to Li Yang the fact that they could communicate easily would be a blessing. She was used to struggling with sign-language and pidgin-English so having a boss with whom she could chat freely would be wonderful.

"Ni hao tai tai," she replied, entering the house, "What a beautiful home."

As Yang cleaned over the next hour she found that her new employer was very open and found out the family's history in a very short period. This was a very new concept to the ayi, as usually it took her months to find out about her foreign bosses, sometimes their secrets becoming a heavy burden.

She learned that her new 'tai tai' was called Chi and she came from Hong Kong, which explained the imperfect Mandarin, as Cantonese would have been the woman's native tongue. Chi was a tiny woman, very delicate in her mannerisms and impeccably dressed with beautiful silky bobbed hair. As Yang stood ironing some shirts in the kitchen, Chi made coffee and explained that she was married to a Greek man called Constantin Helios. They had two young girls aged nine and ten, whom Chi would like Yang to cook dinner for as her last duty of the day.

"I don't cook Chinese food," Mrs. Helios confessed, "But we think it a good idea to introduce the girls to different cuisines. When my husband is home, I cook Greek food for him, you see."

Li Yang nodded, understanding perfectly but she was intrigued to learn more, "You said when your husband is home tai tai...."

"Yes," Chi sighed, pressing down on the cafetiere, "He works away for three months at a time and then comes home for a month. We've got used to it over the years. He used to be based in Hong Kong, that's where we met, but last year Constantin's company moved to Shanghai, so here we are."

The conversation ceased at that point, as two pretty girls came bounding into the house, followed by a young Chinese chauffeur. The children threw their bags into the hallway and raced to hug their mother.

"I fell over and hurt my knee in the playground," the younger girl complained, pulling her lips into a pout, "It's really sore mamma."

"Oh, sweetheart," Chi soothed, rubbing her child's leg, "Would some chocolate milk help?"

The little girl nodded and the pout turned to a smile, "Yes it would!"

Yang listened as she folded one of Mr. Helios' shirts, smiling at the happy environment she was now to become a part of.

"One week tomorrow!" Gregory sang in a baritone voice, "I am sailing, I am sailing...."

"Can't wait," Xu Bo shouted over the top of his friend's melodic tune, "We actually get to look around the ship in the morning. I hope we're assigned a cabin with a good view."

"Imagine, all that sun and fresh air," Dominic, another roommate smirked, "We'll be tanned and eating delicious food every day. What a life, eh?"

Gregory stopped singing and turned to Xu Bo, "Do you think you'll have any more trouble from old Mr. Green? You could lose your position if he says something."

"No chance," the Shanghainese replied confidently, "One word to the local police about our teacher's activities and he'd lose his residency permit. I'll be sailing to paradise with the rest of you."

"Good," the two Filipino's answered in unison, making each other laugh.

"Come on," Xu Bo grinned, "Last class and then we can forget about him forever."

Li Yang's two hours at the Helios home were almost over and she stood washing up the children's dinner plates at the sink, reflecting on what a friendly atmosphere it was. The girls had eaten their steamed fish and mixed vegetable rice without hesitation and the chores that she'd been asked to do were light and not overwhelming. The ayi hoped that Chi needed help for many months to come.

"Well, bye bye," Yang called into the sitting room as she prepared to leave, "See you tomorrow."

"Oh wait a moment," Chi told her, getting up from the sofa with the girls, "Athena and Alysia have drawn pictures for you to take home. Thank you so much for today, I think we'll get along very well."

The ayi stooped to take the drawings that the girls were offering to her, noting that one had drawn a cat while the other had created a family scene of four, with a woman standing to the side which she presumed to be herself.

"Oh, these are beautiful, hen piao lian," she gushed, giving each child a kiss on the cheek, "I'll put them up in my kitchen where I can look at them every day."

Heading outside into the dark night, Yang could see the orange glow of a burning cigarette in the front seat of the Helios' car. It looked as though the chauffeur were still on duty. She gave him a wave and the young man pressed a button to roll down the electric window.

"Everything alright?" he asked, genuinely interested, "Enjoy your first day?"

"Yes, very much," the Shanghainese woman replied, "They seem like a lovely family, how about you? Are you still working? What time do you finish?"

"I'll be off into the city to fetch Mr. Helios shortly," the chauffeur told her, "I should finish around eight."

"Have you worked for them long?" Yang pressed, curiosity getting the better of her.

"A couple of years," the young man answered, finishing his smoke and throwing it into the nearby bushes, "You should get going, it's going to be another frosty night by the look of it. Zai Jian, goodbye."

Yang mounted her scooter and carefully negotiated the winding path between the houses, glad to have found a 'normal' family to work for.

The following day, Xu Bo and the other new recruits stood waiting for the shipping company bus to pick them up. It was a big day for the first-timers as this would be their first experience on board ship and the moment when they'd be assigned to their new semi-permanent homes. They knew that the ship was also the workplace for many long-serving employees too and looked forward to meeting the rest of the crew who hailed from over twenty different countries.

"Yay!" someone shouted as the thirty-two seater pulled up on time, "We're off!"

Xu Bo's parents were working, as they did every other day, totally oblivious to the fact this particular Wednesday marked a significant stage in their son's new career. They had no idea that within a week he would be leaving Shanghai and neither did they realise that it would also bring an end to his sham relationship with Huang Li. In fact, so little did they know, that Li Yang was already planning to take her future daughter-in-law shopping to buy a gown for the wedding. It couldn't be anything too elaborate she told herself, but a traditional Chinese 'qi pao' in embroidered silk would suit the occasion perfectly.

By the time Li Yang arrived at the Helios residence for her second stint, the ayi was full of plans to make her son's upcoming nuptials an event of style and celebration without breaking the bank.

"You look happy today," Chi commented as she popped her head around the door of her husband's study where the new cleaning lady was dusting shelves.

"Oh, tai tai, ni hao," Yang chuckled, stirring from her reverie, "I was thinking about my son's wedding."

"Really? How exciting," her employer gushed, widening her smile, "You must be very pleased."

"You know us Chinese," the ayi continued, "Our only child getting married is a big occasion, although it will certainly cost us a lot of money."

Chi rubbed her chin thoughtfully. She was used to the locals freely discussing their finances, although it was something that the people of Hong Kong certainly wouldn't have done, and wondered if she could help her new employee in some small way. She liked Li Yang's openness and honesty and although it would be wrong of her to offer money at this stage, Mrs. Helios hoped that there was some small way in which she could be of use. She stood listening for a few minutes as Yang reeled off all the necessary purchases for her son's big day and, as she did so, Chi suddenly had an idea.

"You need to buy a silk qi pao?" she repeated, "Maybe I can help."

Gesturing for the ayi to follow her to the master bedroom, Chi Helios entered a huge dressing room with a floor to ceiling walk-in wardrobe. There on far side, was a rail full of traditional Chinese gowns.

"I've had some of these for a long time," Mrs. Helios explained, taking a turquoise and gold qi pao from its hanger, "I was a little bigger in my younger days. What size is your son's girlfriend?"

Li Yang gazed upon the clothes, trying to guess Huang Li's measurements, "She's quite...erm, fat."

Chi giggled at the older woman's forthrightness and searched the rail for a different dress, "This red one is the biggest, the fabric is quite stretchy too. Would you like to take it for the girl to try? I'll never wear it again and it would save you spending money on a new one."

Yang ran a hand over the beautifully embroidered dress, with intricate dragons woven into the cloth, "I really couldn't, this must have been very expensive. Besides, I don't know if it would fit."

Chi nodded and hung the dress back up, "Really, I don't need it. Why don't you bring her over on Saturday? My husband is taking the girls to the zoo as this will be his last weekend before he goes away."

"You're not going?" the ayi queried.

"Oh no, it's their time with daddy," Chi told her, "Constantin will be taking me out for dinner later that night while the girls sleep over at a friend's house."

"Well, if you're sure...." Yang grinned, calculating how much this offer would save her.

"Yes, of course, now off you go it's nearly six. And here's a key in case I'm out when you arrive tomorrow, as I have to go to the school to see Athena's teacher."

The Shanghainese woman took the key and thanked her employer again. How very kind she was.

That night, Li Yang told Xu Wei about her new employer's dress collection and put to him the idea of Huang Li wearing a second-hand dress to her wedding. He didn't seem impressed.

"Do you think the girl will go along with that?" he mumbled, trying to catch the end of the news on television, "Most young women want a brand new gown on the most important day of their life."

"Trust me husband, I'm very good at convincing people what to do for the best."

Xu Bo arrived home just after eight. He was struggling to keep his excitement concealed and went straight into the bathroom to wash his face with cold water before coming out to sit with his parents. The day on board ship had been better than he'd ever expected. The sheer size of the cruise liner had him gazing in awe as the group took their guided tour and even discovering that his shared cabin was internal with no view did nothing to dampen his spirits.

The new recruits had been split into groups according to their respective professions and, belonging to the entertainment sector, Xu Bo, Gregory and Dominic had been taken off to an induction room to meet the rest of their work colleagues. Many of the young men and women in the team had been working on Mediterranean cruises for some years and were glad to see a few new fresh faces. They'd been warm and welcoming, happy to show the trio the ropes.

Meanwhile Huang Li had been checking out the vast array of restaurants with her colleagues and was relieved to find out that she'd be working in the Asian food hall, serving drinks to the customers who would be using the buffet tables and clearing away plates, having to reset quickly for new guests. It all seemed fairly straightforward she contemplated, although the sheer number of passengers was still quite hard to digest. Li wondered where Xu Bo would be working and how close his cabin was to hers, although he'd been spending less and less time with her as the countdown to their venture had begun.

"Ay, Xu Bo," his mother snapped, "Are you even listening to me?"

"What? Sorry," the young man blinked, "I was just thinking about my new job, I start next week."

"Oh good," Xu Wei commented, shifting his backside in the chair, "You'll be earning money again and can contribute something to the wedding."

"Erm, yes, no problem," his son replied slowly, knowing that no such ceremony would actually take place.

"I need Huang Li to come with me on Saturday," Yang continued, "My new boss is going to lend her a qi pao to wear for the big day, it will save us a lot of money."

"Sure, I'll tell her," Xu Bo sighed, not an ounce of emotion reflecting in his features.

"Good, tell her to be here by twelve and we can go directly, do you hear?"

"Yes, yes, no problem. Now I need to get some sleep, I'm shattered." The following day Xu Bo explained his mother's request to Huang Li. "What?" she cried, "No way! I'm not trying on dresses!"

"Look," her friend simpered, putting his head on one side for effect, "It's the very last thing I'll ask you to do, I promise Li. After Saturday we can look forward to getting on the ship and starting our adventures."

"Will I still see you once we're there?" the Dalian native asked hopefully, "We can meet up on our days off, can't we?"

"We'll see," Xu Bo lied, biting his lip and knowing full well that he had no intention of socialising with Huang Li once they'd sailed out of Shanghai. She was simply a means to an end, "We'll be working long hours."

"But we'll have days off," Li pushed, "We could go for walks on deck in the morning sun."

"Whatever Li," the Shanghainese huffed impatiently, "Now, you know what time you need to meet my mother right? Don't be late, this will be the very last time, okay?"

Huang Li nodded and looked up at Xu Bo with watery eyes. She loved him so very much but every day her heart softened, his seemed to harden and his interest lessen. She guessed only time would tell.

On Friday afternoon, Li Yang opened the door to the Helios' home and was welcomed by a scene of chaos. There were suitcases piled up in the hallway and a smart navy uniform hanging on the back of a door. A tall dark-haired foreign man strode back and forth from the study, carrying books and then seeming to change his mind about his choice and going back to change one volume for another.

"Ni hao," she called out tentatively, "Mr. Helios?"

"Ah, you must be Li Yang," the man grinned, stopping in his tracks and holding out a hand, "Here let me help you with that, it's getting a bit stiff in this cold weather."

Yang watched Constantin reach for the heavy door and push it closed with a firm hand. He was a man in his mid-fifties she guessed, at least twenty years older than his wife and bore the leathered skin of someone who had spent much of their youth in the sun. The ayi had never met a person from Greece before and doubted whether she could even pinpoint the country on the map, but she had seen pictures in magazines and knew that it was a place of great beauty with azure waters and white flat-topped houses.

"I'm afraid everywhere is a bit untidy today Yang," the man told her, "I'm packing my things to go away next week. I'm sure my wife explained to you about my job."

"A little," the Shanghainese woman confessed, "You work away." "That's right," Constantin nodded, "I'm the captain of a ship."

"Ship," Li Yang repeated in English, for that was the language in which the two had been conversing due to the Greek's lack of Mandarin, "What is ship?"

Mr. Helios reached for his briefcase and took out a glossy brochure. "Here, I drive this," he laughed, making a steering motion with his hands, "We go all over the world."

Yang took the booklet and stared at the enormous cruise liner pictured on the front, a great many-decked vessel ploughing through blue waves as it traversed the ocean.

"I see," she said, marvelling at the steel giant, "I keep?"

"Yes, yes, go on," Constantin chuckled, "I've got plenty more. Take it home."

"What are you two chatting about?" Chi asked as she came downstairs in running gear, "Ah, I see you've been showing off the ship to Yang. I'm just off to the gym, back by six-thirty darling."

The couple pecked each other on the cheek affectionately and seconds later Chi was out through the door.

"Oi yor," Li Yang chided herself as she attacked a fresh pile of ironing, "I forgot to remind tai tai that I'd be bringing Huang Li to try on dresses tomorrow."

She carefully hung the girl's laundered school shirts in their closets and peeked around the living room door. Mr. Helios was fast asleep on the sofa while Athena and Alysia played with their dolls on the rug beside him.

"Bye bye girls," she whispered, careful not to wake the snoozing man, "See you Monday?"

"Okay," they chimed together, waving frantically as the ayi pulled on her anorak, "Bye bye."

Li Yang closed the door and headed out into the wind, thankful to have such a pleasant position.

The next day, being Saturday, Huang Li arrived on time at her friend's home. Xu Bo ushered her in with hardly a word, being exhausted from his late night shift at the club.

"Remember, be nice and just go along with whatever my mother wants," he hissed, running a hand through his spikey hair, "She's in there."

The young man left Huang Li to face his mother alone, taking himself off to the bathroom and locking the door. Li Yang didn't notice her son's indifference, as she was too excited at the prospect of finding her future daughter-in-law a dress for the ceremony.

"Ni hao," she greeted Li, "Oi yor, I thought I'd seen you with short hair last week. Why on earth did you cut it? Long hair always looks more beautiful on a young woman you know."

Li put a hand up and subconsciously touched her own head, "It's much easier to look after Li Yang. Besides, I needed a change."

The older woman tutted and reached for her coat, "We'd better get going. Let's take the bus and we can chat on the way. It seems you have some explaining to do."

Huang Li looked around desperately for Xu Bo's support but he was still running water and was oblivious to his mother's nagging words, "Okay, I guess."

The bus journey to the Helios residence was a torturous one for the young Dalian native. Xu Bo's mother had obviously chosen the longest route in order to speak her mind about the virtues of saving one's body for the wedding night. There was little that Huang Li could say without giving away their web of deceit, and she sat looking downwards as the older woman hissed quietly in her ear.

"I still think it would be best if you moved in with us for a while after the wedding," Yang was saying, "Maybe for a few months at least. You and Xu Bo need to learn how to live independently and I can show you how to take care of his clothes and cook his favourite dishes."

"Yes, maybe," Li agreed, happy to say anything that would quieten the Shanghainese and stop her from burning the younger woman's ears off with her lecturing, "It might be a good idea."

Yang was pleased with herself and sat for a few minutes with a satisfied expression on her face, her eyes narrowing as she imagined the scenario, "Good girl Huang Li, I'm glad you can see sense."

As soon as the women were safely out through the door, Xu Bo emerged from the bathroom and headed back to the sanctuary of his bedroom. With very few days left until he left the city, the youngster intended to make good use of the empty apartment and began packing the purchases that he'd made over the past few months. Everything would be transferred to Gregory's place that afternoon before his mother returned home, leaving only basic possessions behind.

Xu Bo intended to work his last shift at the club that night and would collect a salary which would have to last him until the first moth aboard ship had been completed. He imagined that there was very little to spend his cash on anyway, with meals being included but he did like a drink now and again which might stretch his limited funds. Just to be on the safe side, Xu Bo intended to ask his father for a loan, one which would eventually get paid back but probably not in person.

"It's just a couple of streets away," Li Yang was telling the girl at her side as they walked away from the bus terminal, "My boss lives in a wonderful white house, bigger than you can imagine."

Li thrust her hands deep into the pockets of her padded coat and buried her face in her scarf.

"What colour dress, do you think you might like for the ceremony?" the older woman asked, "Although I suppose we have to see what will fit you. Perhaps you could lose a few pounds Huang Li?"

The suggestion was met with a scornful look and Xu Bo's mother knew that she had over-stepped the mark. Dear, dear, she told herself, these young women just didn't want to hear the truth.

The pair walked on in silence, each consumed by their own thoughts. Li Yang wishing that her son had chosen a more beautiful and elegant bride, or at the very least one that spoke their Shanghainese dialect, while Huang Li dreamed of digging her toes into the sand of a Spanish beach with Xu Bo sipping a cocktail at her side, his body tanned and lean, hers a good few kilos lighter.

Ten minutes later the women arrived at the housing complex. Li's eyes widened, it seemed that Li Yang hadn't been exaggerating after all, the homes here were incredible. Each had two storeys and a double-garage, and one in particular even had its own servant accommodation at the side. It was to the larger house that the ayi was now pointing, beaming from ear to ear as she did so.

"Look at that," she told Li, spreading her hands wide, "Isn't this a fantastic house? Just like something from an American movie set, and right here in Shanghai."

Gregory pulled the cap off a cold beer as his friend entered the small kitchen, "Is that everything Bo?"

"Pretty much," the Shanghainese man confirmed, "Just a few toiletries and t-shirts left but I can easily fit those into my rucksack on Tuesday."

"Great," the Filipino grinned, "Here you go, last beer for a few days, we need to make sure we don't put on any weight before we start our new jobs or our clothes will be too tight."

Xu Bo nodded, "Yep, I agree. The new stuff felt a bit snug when I tried it on last week. I guess we can use the gym on the ship every day though."

Gregory nodded and helped himself to another bottle from the fridge, "Yeah, it's no big deal. We'll be on our feet for twelve hours a day and will soon burn off any excess fat."

Dominic nudged his way into the kitchen and waved his mobile phone in the air, "One last pizza then guys, before we have to fill our bellies with the culinary delights of the western world?"

Meanwhile Xu Wei was digging over a patch of turf at the Kapoor residence. Something deep in the back of his mind was torturing him, like a niggling itch that he couldn't reach to scratch. It wasn't Xu Bo, he told himself as he toiled with the heavy spade, as his son had been much more amiable over the past few weeks. Neither was it Li Yang. His wife seemed very content at the Percival's, despite the young artist taking much of his inspiration from random inanimate objects, and the couple of hours afterwards with Mrs. Helios seemed to be working out well. For his own part, Xu Bo was happy with his lot. The factory work was steady and paid a regular wage with an annual bonus scheme, as did many of the local Chinese companies in the city. Working here, despite Bibi Kapoor's drinking problem, was therapeutic and earned a nice little sum to add to the pot. No, he pondered, it was something else that wasn't quite right.

Xu Wei leaned on the spade, taking a swig from his flask of tea and rewinding a few days. There, he had it. The person that was bothering him so much was Huang Li. On the day that he and Xu Bo had raced to her apartment there had been no real emotion between the young couple. His son hadn't consoled his bride-to-be, not even a gentle hug or a few words of support for the terrible deed that had been committed by the watcher across the street. The old man twisted the cap back on his flask and stood looking down at the newly dug earth. The strangest occurrence of all, he told himself, was the way in which Xu Bo had later dismissed the incident and refused to report the peeping-tom to the city authorities. Something was very wrong and Xu Wei had a feeling that things were about to go pear-shaped.

Li Yang pushed her key into the lock of Chi Helios's home, ushering Huang Li inside out of the blustering wind and softly closing the door behind her. Faint music came from an upstairs room but the lower rooms in the house remained unoccupied.

"Where is everyone?" Li asked in a low voice as she took in the sumptuous surroundings.

"Oh, I remember," the older lady told her, "Mr. Helios has taken the girls to the zoo today. Tai tai must be upstairs taking a shower or getting changed. She goes to the gym to keep fit you know."

Huang Li recoiled at the very obvious dig at her podgy figure and started to undo her coat. It was warm inside the house and she could feel her cheeks glowing as she stood in the hallway waiting for Yang to decide what to do.

"We can sit in here and wait," the ayi told Li as she led the way into a bright and modern kitchen, "I don't suppose she'll be very long and then we can go up and see which dress will fit you."

The younger woman plonked herself down on a chair and bit at a hangnail. "That's another thing that we'll need to sort out," Yang told the girl, taking out a pocket book to make a note, "We can't have you marrying Xu Bo with your fingernails in that state."

Ten minutes later there was still no sign of Mrs. Helios. Huang Li was getting fed up sitting listening to her friend's mother making plans for the big day and let out a heavy sigh.

"I'm sure she wouldn't mind you going upstairs to tell her we're here," Li sniffed offhandedly.

"Very well," Yang sighed, heaving herself up off the seat, "I'll just be a minute."

As she neared the master bedroom, Li Yang could hear moaning sounds and wondered if her employer were in some kind of trouble, perhaps having fallen and hurt herself, so she pushed gently on the door.

On top of the huge bed, Chi Helios was writhing in ecstasy as a man pushed himself deep inside her, lifting his buttocks to the rhythm of the woman underneath him. Neither noticed the stricken woman watching.

Li Yang tore down the stairs, calling to Huang Li to get her coat, still thinking about Mrs. Helios and that devil of a chauffeur who was committing a terrible deed in his absent master's bed.

Chapter Twelve

Huang Li

Stuffing the letter back into its envelope and then into her pocket, Huang Li sat staring out of the coffee shop window. In two days' time she would be sailing off to a new world and a different life but this piece of correspondence had thrown her a curveball that was totally unexpected. The woman felt a sense of panic wash over her as she watched the busy pedestrians go about their business on the streets. Li breathed deeply to force away the tears that were threatening to come, knowing that the slightest trigger would have them tumbling down her cheeks. She looked around pensively but nobody was taking any notice of the chubby northerner sat in the corner on her own. Time for one more hot chocolate, and perhaps a blueberry muffin, she told herself, just to while away another hour as she decided what to do.

Meanwhile, over in Pudong, Li Yang was just arriving at the Helios' house. It was her first shift since catching her employer with the chauffeur the previous Saturday and she wasn't looking forward to it at all. Her emotions were a muddle of embarrassment, anger and shame but the expression on her face as she opened the front door showed nothing but professionalism. She had no idea what would come out of her mouth, although the ayi had already contemplated confronting Chi Helios, but for the sake of the extra money that was now coming in, Yang had listened to her husband and agreed to keep what she knew to herself. In her husband's book, karma would always find a way to serve revenge on those who sinned.

"Good afternoon Yang," shouted Chi from the living room, where she was sewing labels into the girls gym clothes, "It's a bit warmer outside today isn't it?"

"Ni hao tai tai," the Shanghainese responded curtly, bracing herself for the first sighting of her employer after 'the incident', "Yes, it's not too bad out there today."

"Just think, it's the first of March on Wednesday," the younger woman continued, looking up and smiling as the older lady approached, "And Constantin will be off on his travels again."

"Oh?" Yang managed, she remembered all the suitcases now, "On the ship?"

"Yes, that's right," Mrs. Helios told her, "I tell you what Yang. Would you like to come along with the girls and I? We always go to wave Constantin off when he's going away. It's quite a sight seeing the cruise liner sail out of port with her passengers and crew. They leave at four o'clock, can you make it?"

Li Yang thought for a moment and then agreed, she'd never seen one of those huge ships up close before.

That night, after finalising the arrangements for staying at Gregory's apartment on Tuesday night and picking up his employment papers from the cruise company, Xu Bo made a call to Huang Li.

"I need one last favour," he told her, "I know it's kind of last minute but I think we should go out with my parents for a meal tomorrow, you know, my way of saying goodbye without actually telling them."

There was silence on the other end of the line, prompting him to speak again, "Wei? Li are you there?"

"Yes, I'm here," she sighed, "You know you're not the only one with problems Xu Bo, maybe I have things that I need to take care of before I leave."

"Like what?" he pressed, "Come on Li, just one hour to eat something, that's all I ask."

"And what WILL you tell them?" the woman hissed, "More lies?"

"Just one," he slowly admitted, clicking his tongue as he thought, "I'll tell them that we're going on holiday. That way they won't worry when they don't hear from me for a couple of weeks. As soon as we get to the first port I'll post a letter to them."

Huang Li flinched at the mention of a letter and touched her pocket where her recent postal communication still lay folded inside, "Okay, just an hour Xu Bo, and then that's the end of it."

'Great," the young man chirped, flipping his phone shut, "Good old Li."

On Tuesday morning, Li Yang approached Mr. Percival to see if he'd mind her finishing work early on the following day, so that she could accompany Mrs. Helios and the children to see the ship leave dock.

"Oh, so you like Mrs. Helios better than me do you?" he joked, grinning from ear to ear, but then seeing that the cleaning lady didn't understand the joke, he simmered down, "Of course, go and enjoy yourself."

Yang carried out her chores that day in a sombre mood. She was looking forward to doing something new but being in close proximity to Chi Helios at the moment was not something that she relished the thought of, especially as they'd be riding in the car with that rascal of a chauffeur. Maybe in time she would tell her employer what she'd seen, the woman mused, but in all likelihood she'd keep it to herself.

Yang was stirred from her thoughts by the beep of a message on her mobile phone. Xu Bo was taking them out for dinner tonight, things were looking up.

Huang Li looked at herself in the washroom mirror. She'd made a slight effort with her hair and make-up that night but all her best clothes were packed away ready to transfer to the ship the next day and she had turned up at the restaurant wearing jeans and a plain navy sweater. The look of disapproval on Li Yang's face was a great source of amusement to Xu Bo and his father, but Huang Li had excused herself immediately and headed for the ladies toilet. She took out a pink lipstick and applied another coat, telling herself that as soon as the family had eaten she would make her excuses and leave.

"Huang Li, do you drink wine?" Xu Wei asked as soon as the woman returned to the table.

Li looked at Xu Bo for a clue as to how she should reply but he just shrugged and told his father to order a bottle anyway, one glass wouldn't hurt.

"Listen," the young man announced, placing both hands on the tablecloth in front of him, "Li and I have got something to tell you."

Yang put a napkin up to her mouth, dreading some form of bad news from her only child, "What is it?"

"We've decided to take a holiday. But we're going tomorrow. I got a very good last minute deal."

Xu Wei looked at his wife, hoping that she would take the news with an open mind but unfortunately she was already turning pink and sat back with her arms folded.

"Xu Bo, I am so disappointed in you both. You aren't married yet! It's one thing to be staying out late at night but to go away, and to share a hotel room? Oi yor, this is really very bad indeed."

Huang Li took a couple of large gulps of wine and tried to avoid the older woman's scornful look.

"What do your parents think of this Huang Li?" the Shanghainese lady asked indignantly.

"They don't know," the girl mumbled, heaving her big shoulders up and down. It wasn't a lie, she told herself, as they'd both been dead for over five years. She drank some more wine, emptying the glass.

"Well, I suppose they'll lose their money if they cancel…" Xu Wei commented, trying to ease the tension.

"Exactly!" Xu Bo agreed, glad that his father had come up with a sensible remark, "We have to go now."

"I think we should finish our meal and go home," Li Yang huffed, picking up her chopsticks again.

The little group ate in relative silence until all the plates were cleared.

As they prepared to leave, Xu Bo noticed that Li was a bit unsteady on her feet. Obviously the speed with which she'd been gulping down the wine had made her wobbly.

"Are you alright Li?" he asked, "Let me help you with your coat."

"I'm fine!" the woman snapped, struggling into her jacket, "Just get me a taxi."

As Xu Wei watched the couple rush off through the restaurant's revolving doors, Li Yang was stooping down to pick up something that had dropped from her future daughter-in-law's pocket. It was a plain white envelope with a return address on the back, marked Dalian.

"What's that?" her husband asked, turning around just as Yang put the correspondence into her handbag.

"Huang Li dropped it," she told him, raising her brows, "I'll have to keep it until they come back from their holiday now, won't I? Oh, my goodness husband, youngsters today have no morals at all."

Xu Wei took his wife's arm and walked her over to the exit, "I know my dear, I know."

"What's got into you tonight?" Xu Bo was asking his friend, "You could have been a bit more polite to my mother. Told her how in love with me you are, or something like that."

"Go to Hell Xu Bo," Li retorted, staring out of the cab window, "You know nothing at all."

Xu Bo caught the taxi driver looking at him inquisitively in the rear view mirror and lowered his voice, "Come on Li, it's all over now. You'll never have to see them again. Honestly I don't know why you're so stressed out tonight."

"I'm stressed out because of this," the woman replied, digging a hand into her coat pocket, "Oh no! Where is it? Where's my letter?"

"Your letter?" Xu Bo repeated, "What letter?"

"Arrgghh! I must have dropped it. Never mind, it's none of your business anyway, just drop me on the corner by Starbucks and I'll see you tomorrow."

"As you like," Xu Bo replied calmly, gesturing the driver to stop, "Night Li, see you tomorrow."

Xu Bo had no intention of seeing Huang Li the next day. She'd played her part in his web of lies as far as he was concerned and now that they were embarking on new careers in far off places, he saw no need to fraternise with her. It had,naturally,occurred to the Shanghainese man that his friend might actually be in love with him, but he certainly didn't feel the same way about Li. She was overweight, dowdy and shy, nothing like the people he hung around with on a daily basis. Besides, Xu Bo reflected, Huang Li would be far better off making new acquaintances in her waitressing career.

The following morning, as the sun crept through a gap in the curtains, Li Yang watched her husband scurry off out through the door of their home carrying his crash helmet and a flask of tea. As soon as she heard the latch click shut, the woman padded into the living room in her cotton slippers. She still had another twenty minutes before she had to set off for the Percival's home, just time to open up Huang Li's letter and read the contents inside. With slightly shaking hands, expecting to see an affectionate note from the girl's parents, Yang slid the paper out of its envelope and began deciphering the crudely formed Chinese characters.

'Dear Li, I know where you are and I am coming to bring you home,' she read slowly, 'You made a promise to me and I to you and in the eyes of the law we are united. You have been a disobedient wife but I am willing to forgive you. Before your father died I promised him that I would take care of you. The poor old man's soul would never be at peace if he knew that you had deserted me. You say that I have been harsh with you, but it is a husband's duty to punish his wife if she refuses to serve him. You must agree to change your ways and return to Dalian. My mother is elderly and needs you to cook and clean for the rest of the family. Running away to Shanghai was a foolish move, you knew it was only a matter of time before one of your stupid friends gave the game away. Expect me on March 1st Your husband, Qian.'

Xu Bo's mobile phone vibrated in his pocket as he sat at the back of the bus with his Filipino friends. Looking at it momentarily he saw his mother's number and clicked the device to silent.

"You should get rid of that," Gregory winked, as they arrived at the dock, "New life, new phone. We can afford the latest iPhones now, with our decent salaries and jet-setting lifestyles."

The Shanghainese man looked down at the plastic Nokia in his hand, "You're right," he sighed, opening a side window and deftly throwing the phone into the water, "Out with the old and in with the new!"

Every hour Li Yang stopped her chores and took out her phone, making call after fruitless call to her son.

"Come on, Xu Bo," she muttered under her breath as she heard the operator tell her that a connection couldn't be made, "Where are you?"

At lunchtime, she called Xu Wei and read the letter out to him.

"We have to get hold of Xu Bo," she pleaded, "What time was their flight to Thailand?"

"Oh, I don't think they mentioned it," her husband replied thoughtfully, "Look dear, there's nothing we can do until they return, so please try to calm down."

An hour later as the ayi changed the Percival's bed sheets she felt a familiar vibration in her apron pocket and whipped out her phone immediately, thinking that her son must have finally seen her messages.

"Yang," a familiar voice chirped down the line, "It's Chi. Listen, we can pick you up at three if you give me the address, save you coming over here."

With all the commotion over Huang Li's letter, Yang had forgotten about her arrangement with Mrs. Helios and she was stuck for words as she searched for an excuse not to go.

"Ah, tai tai," she finally managed, "I'm sorry but...."

"Sorry Yang, it's a bad connection, I'm in the car and we're about to go through a tunnel. Text the address to me and we'll see you in a short while."

The Shanghainese woman closed the phone and sighed. It seemed she was going to see the ship leave port today after all.

Huang Li stood at the side of the bus, waiting for the driver to open the luggage hold. She could see Xu Bo and his friends through the window as they made their way down the gangway, laughing and joking, no doubt excited about having arrived at their new home on the water.

"Xu Bo," she called, waving her arm in the air, but the young man gave Li just a cursory glance before turning to chat to his foreign friends.

"I guess I'll see you around then," the woman muttered under her breath as she took hold of her luggage.

Xu Bo looked around the cabin. There wasn't a great deal of space, just two single beds and a couple of built-in wardrobes to store their belongings, but the linen was crisp and the walls were freshly painted. He had been disappointed the previous week, to find that there was no view, no window at all in fact, but he still felt both relieved and excited to finally be on board the cruise liner.

"Shall we go and explore?" Gregory asked, having dumped his bags on top of a bed, "Shall we go and see where we'll be working?"

"Yes, cool," his companion grinned, "Don't forget we have to go and report to our supervisor first."

The pair sloped off, consulting the deck plan as they went. There were so many different levels and passages that they wondered how long it would take them to find their way back to their quarters without the aid of a map.

Passengers were starting to arrive on the upper decks, many of the men dressed in bright Hawaiian style shirts despite the cool March temperature, while almost every woman wore a pair of dark sunglasses, trying to imitate the look of a glamorous star waving goodbye to her fans.

Down on the quay below, and all along the Bund waterfront, hundreds of people were pushing against the barriers, waiting for the moment when the ship's horn was sounded and the tugs guided her out to sea.

Huang Li was happy. Her new roommate was a confident woman, hailing from Shandong Province. This was her third year on the liner, she told Li, and every year it got better. There were many perks and the food was delicious, she confided, just what her new friend wanted to hear. They left the cabin together, chatting about what lay ahead, both eager to see the crowds who had turned out to watch them leave.

Down below, a tall skinny man in his forties was desperately scanning the decks from his poor vantage point on the dockside. There were so many faces looking down from the enormous vessel that after a while they began to merge in his vision. A small boy next to him was holding a pair of binoculars and the man nudged him, asking if he might borrow them for a few minutes.

"Eh?" the child asked, not recognising the Dalian dialect with which the adult spoke, "Ting bu dong."

The man shrugged his shoulders and shuffled along the tarmac, trying to get closer to the ship but he was swayed by the crowd and was forced to regain his former position next to a hydrant, never taking his eyes off the smiling people who looked down from the steel giant.

Captain Constantin Helios stood proudly at the helm, allowing his first mate to carry out some last minute checks before the order was finally given to raise the anchor. The man's pristine uniform, with its shining brass buttons and neatly pressed seams, fitting snugly against his broad muscular chest. Shortly the master of this incredible piece of engineering would step outside onto the upper deck to see if he could spot his wife and children in the family and officials enclosure on the quay. Of course Hu Ping, his driver, would be there too, he acknowledged, standing close to Chi as she waved goodbye for another quarter. It was an amicable arrangement, Constantin admitted to himself, the extra duties that Hu Ping had been willing to administer in his master's absence, taking care of Chi's carnal needs. Of course, his wife had no knowledge that the chauffeur was being paid very well to sleep with her, but neither was she aware of the Captain's torrent of affairs that the hot-blooded Greek needed to satisfy his own cravings during the lonely months at sea. The threat of exposing their agreement had been enough to keep the driver tight-lipped and faithful in his employ. Ten more minutes and he would step out into the dim afternoon sun, ready to wave goodbye to Shanghai.

Li Yang's eyes were opened wide, trying to take in the vast proportions of the cruise liner and the huge number of bodies that sailed on her. Looking at the brochure that Captain Helios had given her, the ayi had never imagined that such a vessel would be capable of taking on board so many people. She had seen the prices too, a pastime for the very rich who had too much time and money on their hands.

Athena and Alysia jumped up and down, suddenly catching a glimpse of their father as he emerged from a doorway on an upper level. Li Yang noticed that Chi was smiling, a genuine look of love that told her that the Hong Kong native would miss her husband during his absence, but the chauffeur was here too, standing stiffly behind them as if awaiting his next instructions.

Yang turned as she heard a man's voice, shouting loudly, trying to be heard above the pandemonium of the excited crowds. He was very tall and waved his arms wildly.

"Huang Li, Huang Li," he cried.

On hearing the familiar name, the Shanghainese woman turned to see who the man was calling to but failed to make out anyone that she recognised. There must be dozens of Chinese with the same name as Xu Bo's girlfriend, she told herself, although it was a strange coincidence that the person calling out her name this time had a distinctly northern appearance and tongue.

"You guys should come out on deck and see the crowds that are here to wave us off," Dominic told Xu Bo and Gregory as they meandered down a hallway away from one of the entertainment areas.

"Where's your cabin?" the Shanghainese asked, "Are you on the same level as us?"

"Next one down," Dominic told him, consulting the deck plan in his friend's hand, "I'm sharing with a guy from Norway, his name's Todd."

"Cool," Gregory jumped in, "What does he do?"

"Works on the cocktail bar," the other Filipino replied casually, "Called himself a mixologist."

The three laughed as they took in the new and unfamiliar profession of Dominic's roommate, this job was going to be full of unexpected surprises.

Huang Li followed her new friend out into the afternoon breeze. The sun was starting to fall behind the Shanghai skyline now and was causing the larger buildings to cast eerie shadows across the water of the Huangpu river's surface. She grabbed hold of the rail and looked down. It was a long way to the dock from up there and the people who stood below looked like tiny colourful buttons in their different spring coats, all waiting patiently for the moment when the ship would depart.

Li turned her head in the wind as she thought she heard a man calling her name, but scanning the crowd, she couldn't make out anyone that she knew, all the faces were blurred and too far away. She breathed in deeply, imagining waking up the next morning without the city smog filling her lungs.

The woman from Dalian yearned to know where Xu Bo's cabin was and who he was sharing with. She was going to miss him, despite their friendship being very one-sided. She could see that now, the man had used her and she'd been a fool to go along with it. Never mind, Huang Li told herself as she stood letting the wind whip at her hair, nothing was as bad as living with Qian. Her father forcing her to marry her much older cousin had been a curse. The man was dirty and crude, expecting Li to work from dawn to dusk in his mother's shabby home that they shared with nine other members of the family. Lying next to him every night had been traumatising. The man seldom washed and many of his yellowing teeth were missing. Qian also liked to drink and use his wife as a punch bag, the final straw that had forced her to make the decision to hitch her way to Shanghai, taking many perilous routes and many months. Now, at last, she was safe.

Li Yang pulled her phone out and pressed Xu Bo's number for the twelfth time that day. Still no signal. Chi looked at the ayi enquiringly, watching her employee slip the object back into her pocket.

"Is everything alright Yang?" she asked kindly, her eyes still searching the upper decks for a last sighting of Captain Helios, "Is something wrong?"

"No, tai tai," Li Yang shook her head, "Mei wen ti, no problem."

Yang knew that Xu Wei would be worrying too, but he always seemed to have a much more practical approach to their family problems. All those months worrying about their son's whereabouts and in the end her husband had been right in his assumption that the young man had found a girlfriend. Finding out that Huang Li was married was something different altogether though, she worried deeply about Xu Bo's future and the intricate web that the Dalian woman was weaving around him.

Qian turned his collar up against the biting breeze that had suddenly blown upstream. He was certain that he could see Huang Li on one of the upper decks, but she looked different now, shorter hair and more confident than she had ever been in his presence.

"Huang Li," Qian shouted again, his voice failing to carry the distance to where his wife now stood looking down into the crowd, "I want you to come home."

"Sir you need to step back," an official told the Dalian citizen, "You can't come any closer."

Qian looked down and found that he had subconsciously walked to the edge of the barrier and his feet were now touching the plastic luggage ramp that stood idle at the edge of the dock.

"My wife," he managed pointing to where, up until a few seconds ago, Huang Li had been gazing down.

"Sorry sir, you don't have an official pass, now please, step back."

"Mu hou er guan," Qian spat at the petty official, "You're a monkey in a tall hat."

Seconds later, the man felt himself seized from behind and escorted off the quayside, struggling against the officers who dragged him away to be cautioned at the police station.

"Filth," tutted the official, straightening his cap, "Bloody northerners."

Finally the horn sounded. Two tugs led the way as the sleek white liner softly moved through the waters and out towards the China Sea. A roar went up in the crowd, some people staying to watch the full departure while others began to wander off towards their homes, chattering excitedly about all that they'd seen as the sea vessel pressed on up river.

Captain Helios stood proud, his back stiff and his eyes fixed straight ahead as the Nanpu Bridge became a mere matchstick structure behind them. A faint purple glow was painted upon the horizon now, tinged with pink and orange, a fair sign that the skies would be clear that night.

Li Yang followed Chi and the children back to the car parked some streets away. Hu Ping had gone on ahead to warm the engine, obviously in a hurry to get his mistress home again. She tried Xu Bo's phone one last time before climbing into the back of the sedan, still unable to get through to her precious son. All that could be done now was to wait until the couple returned from their holiday in a couple of weeks, she told herself resignedly, and then Huang Li had better have a very good explanation.

Xu Wei sat at the kitchen table waiting for his wife to come home. He knew that there would be trouble when he confessed to her that he'd felt something strange about Xu Bo's relationship. She was bound to reprimand him for not raising his fears earlier and, as he sat there playing out the scenario in his mind,

Xu Wei took out a bottle of mao tai Chinese spirit from the back of the cabinet and poured himself a glass. I might as well be prepared, he sighed.

Huang Li returned to her cabin to change into her smart new waitress uniform. It was a little snug, perhaps due to the excessive amount of hot chocolate and muffins that she'd consumed over the past few weeks, but no matter, she was here, on board and looking forward to a bright future.

Epilogue

Gizelle leaned forward to apply crimson lipstick under the bright electric bulbs of her dressing table. She wore a red silk robe, open just enough to reveal a matching lace bra and panties. Behind her, on a clothes rail, hung the velour leopard-print gown that she intended to wear for the first part of tonight's show.

The schedule was tougher than the young woman had expected, having to change costumes six times for each set and learn a new dance routine every few days. The pounds had started dropping off already but she loved the buzz of being the centre of attention and the loss of weight had only enhanced her hip bones and already shapely legs.

"Have we shaved girls?" the director asked, cheekily running a finger along one dancer's thigh, "We don't want to see any dark hairs poking out from places where they shouldn't be."

Gizelle put a hand down to check her own legs, satisfied that she had already removed any unwanted strands, but also knowing that Jet would be keeping a close eye on the personal housekeeping of his girls.

"Right, who's up first?" the dance instructor called, "Mimi, Gizelle, chop chop."

Sliding the soft fabric down over her slim frame, the dancer smoothed her dress and slipped both feet into six-inch heels, uncomfortable but so, so glamorous.

All eyes were upon the two dancers as they mimed to a Shirley Bassey song while strutting across the stage. Everyone turned to the side curtains as another, more mature, figure made a grand entrance, performing a song for real, her vocal chords more than capable of pulling off a good rendition.

Another six sets and the girls were finally finished for the night, handing the reins over to a male troupe who sang Western pop music and sixties classics, quickly changing their look from sailor uniforms to cowboy outfits in the blink of an eye.

The crowds were loving their first week's entertainment, sure that this was just a taste of what was to come on their amazing cruise. The flamboyant costumes, dramatic back-drops and free-flowing booze did much to heighten spirits, giving the over-seeing Captain Helios a great deal to be proud of as he toured the different decks, checking that all was well with the passengers in his care.

Having finished her show, Gizelle carefully peeled off the false eyelashes that were a key part of her make-up, wincing as they snagged on her upper lids. She had already discarded the tightly-fitting shoes and now turned her attention to rubbing lotion on her toes, trying to keep them supple and blister free.

"We did alright didn't we?" Mimi smiled at the next dressing-table as she wiped off a patch of orange-hued foundation, "I'm loving those old Motown numbers."

Gizelle nodded and stretched her long legs out until they were resting on the table top in front of her.

"When do we get to the first port?" she asked looking sideways at her friend, "Any idea?"

"The day after tomorrow," Mimi confirmed, looking up at a calendar on the wall of their dressing-room, "Why? Do you need to post that letter?"

Gizelle sighed and peeled off her long dark wig, revealing short spikey hair underneath, "Well, I guess I owe it to my parents don't I?"

"Aw, Xu Bo," the other dancer sighed.

"Hey," Gizelle shot back, "Don't call me that okay. I'm never going to be Xu Bo, not ever again."

"Sorry, a slip of the tongue," Gregory replied in his high-pitched Mimi voice, "But what are you going to tell them? Will you tell them the truth?"

"Hah," the Shanghainese gasped, "What? That their only son has become an exotic dancer and dresses as a woman six nights a week? What do you think?"

"But then there's no turning back..." his friend started.

"No, there isn't. Xu Bo died on that dockside in Shanghai, Gizelle is here to stay."

About the Author

Having been brought up in a small village in the English countryside, A.J.Griffiths-Jones has plenty of happy memories from which to source information for her novels. However, it's been a long journey. Spanning three decades and two continents, her career & personal life have taken some incredible turns, finally bringing A.J. back to her roots and a promising writing career.

As a young woman, A.J. left the rolling Shropshire hills behind her & headed to London, where she became fascinated in the world of Victorian crime & in particular the unsolved case of 'Jack the Ripper'. Having read every book available to her on the subject, she started her own mini investigation which eventually led to her first non-fiction publication. However, there was a long period of research necessary before A.J. could finally complete her first book and during the intervening years she relocated to China with her husband and took up a post as Language Training Manager for an International bank. As the need for English grew within the company, A.J's responsibilities expanded until she was liasing between two cities and nearly three thousand employees. An initial two year move soon turned into a decade and the couple found themselves in the vast metropolis of Shanghai for a much longer period than they had firstly intended.

Using their Asian home as a base, A.J. and her better half travelled extensively during their time overseas, visiting New Zealand, Australia, Philippines, Malaysia, Thailand and many provinces within China itself At weekends they would jump into their Jeep and set off to remote villages and mountains, armed with little more than a compass and a map set in Chinese characters, photographing their trip as they explored. Eventually the desire to move back to the U.K. prevailed and the couple returned to their native land in 2012. It was at this point that A.J. made the decision to fulfill her lifetime ambition of becoming an author.

Initially embarking on penmanship in the historical crime genre, A.J. felt it necessary to create a balance between research and writing. The long hours of studying census reports and old newspapers were beginning to take their toll and, having a natural ability to see the funny side of everything, she decided to turn her hand to writing suspense novels with a comical twist. This newfound combination of writing styles has enabled A.J. to get the best of both worlds. For half of her working week she creates humorous characters in idealic locations, whilst the rest of her hours are devoted to research in the Victorian era.

In her free time, A.J.Griffiths-Jones is a keen gardener, growing her own produce and creating unique recipes which she regularly cooks for friends & family. Her plan is to create healthy, filling meals which will eventually be compiled into a cookbook. In her free time A.J. still enjoys travelling, although these days she spends her time visiting Europe and the British Isles, and takes regular holidays in Turkey where she has a relaxing holiday home, which also serves as a haven to complete the final chapters in her books with a glass of wine and a beautiful sunset.

Another of the author's passion's is reading, especially books that take her out of her comfort zone and into a different historical period.

Nowadays, A.J. lives in a Shropshire market town with her husband and beloved Chinese cat, Humphrey. She regularly gives talks at local venues and has also appeared as a guest speaker at New Scotland Yard, where her investigative research was well-received by the Metropolitan Police Historical Society. The author's professional plan is to write a series of suspense novels as well as non-fiction publications relating to notorious historical figures.

Lightning Source UK Ltd.
Milton Keynes UK
UKHW020957291121
394778UK00011B/1014